The Viscount Says Yes

The Viscount Says Yes

A Meddle & Mend Epilogue

By

Sarah Wallace

CONTENTS

Content Warning ... ix

Prologue ... 1
Day One ... 5
Day Two ... 13
Day Three ... 28
Day Four ... 43
Day Five ... 77
Day Six ... 99
Day Seven ... 119
Note from the Author ... 132
Acknowledgments ... 135
About the Author ... 137
Also by Sarah Wallace ... 139
Sign up for my newsletter! ... 141
Preview for Breeze Spells and Bridegrooms ... 142

For those who need the reminder: you are loved.
This book is for you.

CONTENT WARNING

The Viscount Says Yes is a soft epilogue with low conflict. However, there are references to past abuse experienced by the main character, including sexual abuse, grooming, and trafficking.

PROLOGUE

Pip Standish sat straight in his seat. The sun shone through the stained-glass windows, casting a rainbow of color across the church and onto the happy couple exchanging their wedding vows. Pip basked in the glow of the sunlight, the warmth of the love on display, and the security found in being surrounded by loved ones. He smiled wide enough to dimple his cheeks.

Gerry looked lovely as always in a sprigged muslin gown. She had small white flowers in her light red hair, tucking the stems into her updo so the buds looked like little pearls. Basil beamed at his bride, looking equal parts fit to burst and as though he hardly dared believe she was real. When they were pronounced husband and wife, Gerry tugged Basil's lapels so she could kiss him. He seemed only too happy to oblige.

The little church in Tutting-on-Cress had already hosted a Hartford wedding, but Gerry's wedding to Basil Thorne was a good deal more boisterous than when Gavin married Charles Kentworthy. After all, Basil Thorne came with a whole collection of half-siblings. The Thorne children tended to take over situations. Pip rather liked it. He preferred to not be the center of attention. This wasn't to say he was overlooked when the children were around—his friends always seemed to be highly aware of his presence and careful with his comfort—but the focus was never on him. While he knew one or two of the older children thought him attractive, they were always too shy to make him uncomfortable. He was able to relax around them, and he found that discussing what the children found interesting was often easier discourse than what most adults wanted to discuss.

After the wedding concluded, close friends and family went to the Thorne home for breakfast. It was a noisy affair, with everyone chatting and laughing. Pip found a settee in a corner of the room and allowed the joy of the gathering to wash over him. Little Grace Thorne found him and asked shyly if she might sit with him. He obligingly moved over to give her space and they sat together, quietly observing everyone around them. Pip adored it.

When the celebration was winding down, Charles and Gavin found him and they all walked home together. Seb, Gavin's younger brother, walked home with his betrothed, Laurence Ayles, to spend the rest of the day at Copperage Farm.

When they sat down to dinner, Gavin said it first. "God's teeth, it's strange to not have Gerry here anymore."

Pip nodded feelingly. "I'm glad Seb will still be here to walk to the village," he said. "It would be too odd walking to the shop alone."

Charles smiled at him. "If you ever want company for the trip, darling, you know you need only ask."

Pip was not at all sure he'd ever feel comfortable asking for such a thing, so he said nothing.

"And," Charles went on, "you have a week before the shop reopens. So that will give us all some time to acclimatize." He glanced at his husband, who still looked disgruntled. Charles picked up Gavin's hand and kissed the inside of his wrist, which effectively cleared Gavin's prickly expression.

Pip sagged a little in his chair. "I wish she hadn't needed to close the shop," he admitted. "But I still can't imagine running it without her."

It had been decided, after much deliberation, that Gerry's spell shop would close for a week while she and Basil went to Bath for their honeymoon. Several people tried to push the couple to extend their holiday, but Gerry could not bear to be so long from her business, and Basil could not bear to be so long from his family.

Gerry had taught Pip to restock inventory, but he did not know how to assemble all of the spellbags they carried. As usual, she sensed Pip's discomfort with the notion. In the end, she declared they would announce a week-long closure, and she stocked up on everything in preparation. Word went out and the community responded, buying all the spells they thought they might need while Gerry was away. It had been enjoyable to be so completely busy for the fortnight leading up to the wedding. Pip barely had time to think about the changes to come.

Now Gerry was married and off on her honeymoon. The house felt empty without her, even though it still contained four people. Pip was sure they would see little of Seb during the shop's week-long closure. Laurence was back at home for a short while, and the two planned to devote as much time as possible to working on Laurence's garden expansion. Pip anticipated a great deal of time alone in the days ahead and he was not looking forward to it.

DAY ONE

Pip turned out to be only partially correct. Charles and Gavin each invited him to join them for walks in the garden and rides around the estate. But halfway through the day after Gerry's wedding, Pip was already decidedly restless and dreading another quiet dinner at home.

"I think I might go visit Bertie for tea," he said after lunch.

Charles did not seem surprised. "Certainly, darling. Shall I send round the carriage?"

"No, thank you. I like the walk."

After spending most of his life in London, Pip had come to adore long walks in the country. It alarmed him when he first moved to Tutting-on-Cress: the wide-open spaces, the rolling hills, the woods and streams. Now, he relished the openness and the quiet unique to nature.

He found Viscount Bertie Finlington in his study. Pip was so regularly a guest at the large manor that the footman no longer announced him; he simply took Pip's things and advised him as to where Bertie was located. Pip suspected it was a standing instruction. He quite liked it.

He paused for a moment on the threshold to the study,

admiring the view of the viscount sitting at his desk. He couldn't see what Bertie was working on, but he thought it must be something complex, as the gentleman looked very focused. Pip warmed at the sight. He had the sudden desire to surprise Bertie by kissing him on the cheek.

But he didn't act in time. Bertie registered Pip's presence and looked up with a grin and a "Good afternoon, petal!" Pip smiled broadly.

Bertie stood and came out to greet him. Pip had a brief regret that he hadn't taken the opportunity to move first. Then again, he never had the courage to kiss Bertie, even as innocently as on his cheek. He kept fearing he wouldn't be ready for such a thing. But the notion to kiss the other man had been coming up more and more in his imagination lately. He stowed the thought away as Bertie led him into the room.

"Would you like some tea, darling?"

"That would be lovely, thank you."

"Why don't we go into the sitting room then? More comfortable seats, I fancy."

Pip nodded and took Bertie's hand. It had been two years since Pip had come to live in Tutting-on-Cress, and Bertie still took great care never to initiate contact. Pip adored him for it. And though Pip had grown progressively more comfortable with taking Bertie by the hand and leaning his head on Bertie's shoulder, his friend never presumed and always let Pip be the one to decide. It was blessedly freeing—but then, Bertie was a blessedly freeing person to be around anyway. The only problem was that this meant it was up to Pip to push things along. While he was grateful for the control, he felt anxious about it.

In an effort to distract himself from such thoughts, he said, "What were you working on?"

"Calculations. I'm designing a new tool for magic. Should be exciting when it is all finished, but it is dashed complicated."

"You looked very focused."

Bertie smiled. "Yes, it's a good thing you came in when you did. I don't think I've moved from my desk since I sat down this morning."

"You haven't had lunch?"

Bertie gave a little shrug. "Oh, I had something brought to me. I didn't want to stop what I was doing, you know."

Pip hmphed in response. Bertie was so good about taking care of other people, it never occurred to Pip that he was not always good at taking care of himself. He hated the prospect.

Bertie seemed to read his thoughts for he gave Pip a sidelong glance as he rang for tea. "You needn't fret, darling. Most days I have Seb here, so the company encourages me to move about. Sweet Seb is so restless, I'm often giving us both something active to do in order to help with that."

"Seb said you gave him the week off," Pip said as they sat down on their favorite settee.

"Yes, well, I thought he'd appreciate it, what with Laury in town and everything. Is the dear boy ever at home these days?"

"Of course he isn't." Pip covered Bertie's hand with both of his. "And you're deflecting. Don't think I didn't notice."

Bertie chuckled. "You darling man. Are you worried for me?"

"Shouldn't I be?"

"Well, I confess I'm not accustomed to it. I'm so used to my own ways and my own company, you know. The only people who fret over me are Charlie, Julian, and my mother."

"Perhaps you need looking after," Pip said softly.

Bertie looked fond. "Undoubtedly, petal."

Pip thought he *might* be on the verge of having the courage to *consider* kissing Bertie then, only the tea trolley was brought in at that moment.

"So," Bertie said as he poured out. "How do you plan to spend this week while Gerry is away?"

He was deflecting again. Pip decided to let him. Bertie rarely talked about himself. "I'm not at all sure," he said. He accepted the teacup and took a sip. "So don't be surprised if I find my way here every day."

Bertie gave him a huge smile. "That would be delightful, darling. I look forward to it. Shall we do anything particular with all that extra time?"

Pip felt himself flush, thinking for a moment that Bertie was being indelicate. But then he realized Bertie was never indelicate, so he gathered himself together and said, "Did you have something in mind?"

"Well," Bertie said, stirring his tea thoughtfully. "It does seem like an excellent time to have a go at that quizzing glass."

Pip stared. "You mean haven't worked on it yet?"

It had been over a year since Pip had seen the quizzing glass in question, when his former employer and lover, Jack Reid, had attempted to steal it, using Pip to do so. It was the same quizzing glass that had thrown Pip and Bertie together in the first place; Jack had sent Pip and his friend Nell to steal it from Bertie. Bertie had been very gracious about the whole thing. He hadn't called the magistrate and had simply sent Pip and Nell on their way. He was not quite so gracious with Jack, much to Pip's relief.

"No, my sweet. I was waiting for you."

"Oh," Pip said. "You needn't have."

"It was no hardship. I'm quite looking forward to working on it with you."

"But it's been—I don't even know how long. Years?"

Bertie chuckled. "It's not going anywhere. I'm not going anywhere. There's no hurry, Pip."

Bertie so rarely said his name that Pip took a moment to

consider his words. "I know," he said at last. He heaved a sigh. "You've been so patient with me. And I'm sure you know how much I appreciate it. But," he said, setting his cup aside. "I wish I didn't need your patience so very much."

Bertie set his own cup aside and held out his hand, an invitation, not a demand. It was never a demand with Bertie.

Pip accepted the invitation, sliding his own hand into his friend's.

"We have all the time in the world, darling," Bertie said gently. "Years and years."

Pip turned so he could lean his head on Bertie's shoulder. "I feel as though my past keeps holding me back from my future."

Bertie squeezed his hand. "What you went through was no small thing. Give yourself some grace to heal from it."

Pip nodded but didn't sit up. As usual, Bertie didn't rush him. He never rushed him. They sat in companionable silence for a long while. Finally, Pip sat up and picked up his tea. The tea in the cup was cold, but that never bothered him much.

Bertie tsked as Pip drank his cold tea in one gulp. "Oh, I do wish you'd let me get you a new cup."

"And waste perfectly good tea?"

Bertie chuckled. "So, shall we make a project of the quizzing glass then?"

"Yes. It sounds like a splendid way to spend the time."

"Delightful! I'm not sure I'll be able to start today. I have to prepare some ingredients and tools for testing, you see. But we can start tomorrow, whenever you'd like."

"Thank you," Pip said. "I'll trot around some time after breakfast."

Bertie poured him another cup of tea. "As ever, darling, this house is always open to you. Don't fret about coming too early and don't fret about keeping me waiting. I'm quite happily at your disposal."

Pip smiled and, before he could get himself fussed about it, he leaned forward and kissed Bertie on the cheek. "Thank you, Bertie."

Bertie's reaction was most gratifying. The gentleman blushed becomingly and looked a little flustered. "Good heavens," he said as he took a sip of tea. "You sweet thing."

The adorable reaction charmed Pip more than he might have expected. He found it was thrilling too, to kiss Bertie's cheek because *he* wanted to, not because he had been made to. Perhaps showing more affection would not be quite so difficult as he had thought.

They spent the rest of the afternoon chatting amiably about nothing. Bertie invited Pip to stay for dinner and Pip accepted. It was a dance with which they were both well-versed. When Gavin and Gerry's relations had come to stay for a long visit, Pip took to spending a great deal of time at Bertie's house. Like that evening, it had been in part an escape from home, only then it had been from uncomfortable conversations and terse exchanges, rather than quiet. After dinner, they had a bit of port and then Bertie sent Pip home in his carriage. Pip did not kiss Bertie good night, although he did consider it. He supposed, as the carriage rattled down the road, that it was something to work up to.

Charles and Gavin were waiting up for him in their usual manner—which is to say, they were trying to look like they weren't waiting up for him, and acted surprised that he had come home at all. They were sitting as they often did of an evening, together on a sofa with Charles leaning against the corner of the sofa and Gavin leaning against Charles. Gavin was reading a book with Charles reading over his shoulder. It was an endearing sight and it occurred to Pip that it was likely how they would spend their evenings when the house was empty and theirs alone.

"Good evening, darling," Charles greeted him. "Did you have a pleasant time?"

"Oh, yes," Pip said. "Always nice to visit. I...er...imagine I'll be visiting quite a lot this week."

Charles smiled knowingly. "I would have expected no differently. And how did you leave Bertie?"

"He is well," Pip said, taking a seat in a plump easy chair. He hesitated for a moment and then, because Bertie had mentioned Charles earlier, decided to be honest about some of his concerns. "Do you know whether Bertie is in the habit of... neglecting himself?"

Charles frowned a little. "What do you mean, darling?"

"Well, he said he hadn't moved from his desk since breakfast. And that he'd only eaten lunch because it was brought to him."

Charles huffed. "Ah, yes. A bad habit, I'm afraid. He does get lost in his work."

Pip considered. "I suppose he had Nell to keep him from doing that for a bit, and then Seb as well...not to mention that month or so with the applicants living there," he added, thinking of the half-dozen spellcasters who had stayed in Bertie's home as he determined who would be the best fit as the new Royal Spellcaster to the Crown.

"It worries you?" Charles said.

"I suppose it never occurred to me that he might not look after himself. He's always so good at looking after other people."

"Indeed. Well, if you intend to go there every day, I'm sure you will keep a proper eye on him."

Pip had a feeling Charles was teasing him.

Gavin leaned back into Charles a bit. "Stop teasing him, Charles."

Charles's smile broadened and he ran a hand through Gavin's hair. "I think our Pip knows it's all out of love."

Pip was distracted momentarily by the show of affection. The prospect of having a hand in his hair used to horrify him—too many ugly memories—but he realized, suddenly, that he felt a little wistful at the sight. He shook himself mentally.

"I do," he assured Charles. "Anyway, just curious to know if it was a new habit or not. I shall be on the watch for it."

DAY TWO

The next morning, Pip joined Charles, Gavin, and Seb at the breakfast table. When he walked into the room, he realized he was walking into the middle of a somewhat heated discussion.

"Didn't he say this would be his last long trip for a while?" Gavin said.

Seb huffed. "Yes. He did."

"Then why do you not wait until he returns, darling?" Charles said.

"Because I don't want to wait."

"And what does he want?"

Seb looked sullen. "Laury wants to wait."

Gavin raised his eyebrows expressively.

"I *know*. And I know he said it would take a while. And I know we said we'd make it a long engagement. And I know when he proposed he said he was happy to wait for as long as we both needed. But...well, hang it all, *you* only waited a year."

"We were both older," Gavin said. "It was a little different."

"And neither of us were starting new careers," Charles said.

Seb leaned his cheek on his hand. Pip quietly got his food,

wishing he hadn't walked in when he did. But it was, of course, far too late now.

"Are you sure this isn't because Gerry is married?" Gavin said in his quiet, solemn way.

Seb sighed. "Course it isn't." He paused. "Although I *am* miffed that I got engaged before she did and then she went and got married before me."

"It is not a race," Charles said.

"I know, and if it were I'd have lost anyway."

Gavin rolled his eyes.

"How are you this morning, darling?" Charles said as Pip sat down.

"I am well, thank you," he said. "How is everyone doing today?"

Gavin poured Pip a cup of tea. Pip was struck quite suddenly with the question of whether such a responsibility would ever fall to him—not in this household, of course, but perhaps in another house. He wondered if he was doing the same thing as Seb, taking Gerry's marriage as a sort of cue.

"We're doing quite well," Gavin said. "Although Seb is in high dudgeon—"

"I am not!"

"—as you can see."

"Anything the matter, Seb?" Pip said carefully.

Seb heaved another sigh. "I was only saying that I rather think Laury and I should get married before he goes back to London. But they both think I shouldn't. And Laury thinks we shouldn't. As a matter of fact, everyone thinks we shouldn't except me. But I don't see how it's such a spectacular idea. We are engaged, after all."

Pip very cautiously said nothing.

"I suppose you agree with them," Seb said, sounding mulish.

"Perhaps we can talk after breakfast," Pip ventured. "It might help to sort out your thoughts."

Seb brightened considerably. "Yes. Thank you. I think that would help."

Pip nodded, satisfied. His friendship with Seb was a very unique one. He had never before had a friend who looked up to him. For most of his life, people had looked down on him. His only friend growing up, though younger than he, had acted as his protector for too long to consider him any sort of role model. And his ex-lover had been considerably older, not to mention cruel—he certainly never thought of Pip with any sort of respect. The Dukex of Molbury treated him like an adopted child. And while Charles, Gavin, and Gerry all treated him with the utmost respect and care, Pip always felt like an adopted younger sibling.

He treasured it—having a sort of family at last. But he treasured his friendship with Seb for entirely different reasons because Seb came to him for advice. It had alarmed him at first, to be thought of as an expert on anything. But Seb was so earnest and so genuine and he listened so well that Pip found himself enjoying the role far more than he would have expected. It made him feel even more a part of the family to have something akin to a younger brother.

After breakfast, they walked out into the garden together.

"So," Pip started. "Why don't you tell me why you're so eager?"

Seb was all tension, shoving his hands into his pockets and kicking at pebbles as he talked. Seb was like that. His moods and emotions were always written all over him. Pip rather liked the forthrightness of it. "I don't know if I can explain it. I know it's stupid. And I know there's no hurry. But I feel as if we've been engaged for ages. And—" He broke off, blushing.

"And?" Pip prompted.

"And there's a small stupid part of me that is worried if we don't get married soon, we'll never do it. We'll only talk about it."

"Do you really think Laurence would do such a thing to you?"

Seb huffed. "No, I suppose not. But what if he realizes that he travels to London too much and that he shouldn't get married at all?"

"How long will he be gone?"

"Another month."

"And when he gets back, how long will he stay?"

"Three months."

Pip did not speak right away. Finally, he said, "If I remember correctly, he usually stays in London longer and at home for briefer periods. This seems a desirable change to that previous pattern."

"That's what he said too. He said it would be a better way to start the marriage, with us living together for three months."

"I'm inclined to agree with him. What bothers you about it?"

"I don't know. I thought it might be nice for him to come home to a husband, you know?"

Pip stopped so he could turn to look at his friend.

Seb's forehead was crinkled with frustration. "I cannot stand an entire month with the house being so quiet," he said, as if the words were bursting out of him. "It is too strange having Gerry gone."

Pip smiled sympathetically. "It is, isn't it?"

"I'm glad you understand at least."

"I do. And I also think you would not be happy if you got married before Laurence left for London."

Seb kicked at a pebble again. "Why not?"

"Because it would be too strange to be at Copperage Farm without him."

Seb let out a long breath. "You're right," he said quietly. "I hadn't thought of that."

"And do you really believe he will change his mind?"

"No, of course he wouldn't. Only..."

"Only?"

Seb frowned at the ground and kicked at a pebble again, avoiding eye contact. "When he proposed, he said he wanted to spend the rest of my life with me, but didn't care when the rest of his life began." He looked up at Pip, his expression tight with worry. "But I do. Care, I mean. I want the rest of my life to begin right now. Is that so very awful?"

This was such a mirror of his own turbulent thoughts that Pip was quite struck for a moment. Finally, he gathered his wits and said, "Of course it isn't. And I daresay it is very understandable. But is a month such a very long time to wait? As I understand it, getting married quickly is very difficult."

Seb looked at the ground again. "I know. It is. And you're right. It isn't so very long. Thank you," he mumbled.

Pip smiled to himself and put a hand on Seb's shoulder. "How long do you have before he leaves again?"

"A fortnight."

"Then perhaps you ought to take advantage of every moment before then?"

Seb nodded, a quick, brief nod—more to himself than anything else. "Right. Thanks, Pip." He hurried off.

Pip watched him walk away and then did a slow circuit of the garden alone, mulling over the conversation. Then he went back inside to inform the Kentworthys he was leaving. He found them both in Charles's study. Charles was sitting at his desk and Gavin was sitting on the desk, facing him. Charles had a hand on his husband's leg. As they had the night before, they looked adorably domestic. Pip smiled at the sight, feeling a small pang.

Charles saw him first. "Off to Bertie's again?"

Pip leaned against the doorjamb. "I know I don't need your permission or anything. But I don't like to disappear without telling anyone."

Charles smiled. "I certainly appreciate it."

"Did you get Seb straightened out?" Gavin asked, turning on the desk to look at him.

"I think so."

"I'm glad you could talk some sense into him," Gavin said.

Pip shrugged. "I can relate a bit to his concerns."

Charles looked at him consideringly. "Indeed? Do you want to talk about it?"

Pip chuckled. "Probably. But not quite yet."

"Very good. But you do know that either of us or both of us are available any time you need?"

"I do," Pip said. "Thank you."

With that, he left and took the lovely, long walk to Bertie's house.

He found Bertie in his study again, looking as serious and focused as he had the day before. Remembering his own regret at not acting sooner the previous day, Pip listened to his instincts and strolled into the room before he had the chance to doubt himself.

"Good morning, my darling," Bertie said, setting aside his pen.

Feeling bold, Pip perched on the edge of Bertie's desk, like Gavin had done. He felt a bit terrified at the forwardness, but Bertie looked inordinately pleased by it.

"Well," Bertie said, beaming up at him. "This is quite delightful."

And because it was Bertie, Pip felt comfortable being honest. "I thought I would try it and see how it felt."

Bertie's smile broadened. "I can tell you, I thoroughly enjoy it." He tilted his head. "How are you finding it?"

Pip considered. "I think I like it."

"Excellent!"

Pip picked up Bertie's hand where it rested beside his leg. "Did you have breakfast?"

Bertie chuckled. "I hope you're not still worried about me, m'dear."

Pip raised an eyebrow but did not say anything. He rested his hand, still holding Bertie's, on his lap.

Bertie blushed and shifted in his seat. "You really needn't fret. I have a wonderful staff. They ensure I eat."

From his new vantage point, Pip could see that Bertie's blush went down his neck. This discovery led to intriguing thoughts of whether Bertie blushed elsewhere. Pip swiftly squashed that thought. It wouldn't do to think of it now, sitting where he was. "I'm sure they do their best," he said. "But I'm not sure they would be able to make you eat if you're skipping meals."

"Oh, darling, I don't like you worrying about me."

Since he was already being bold, and rather liking it, Pip decided to continue with the theme. He reached up with his other hand and cupped Bertie's cheek.

Bertie's blush deepened.

Pip leaned forward a little—not enough to offer a kiss, but enough to speak softly. "Then please take care of yourself. Charles says that skipping meals is an old habit."

Bertie huffed. "He did, did he?"

Pip rubbed his thumb gently against Bertie's temple and he leaned forward a little more.

"Please promise me you will work on it."

Bertie's gray eyes were fixed on his. He leaned his head ever so slightly into Pip's hand. "I promise."

Pip rather wanted to run his hand through Bertie's lovely light brown hair, but he wasn't sure he was ready for that. Besides, he'd tried enough boldness for one morning. Perhaps hair ruffles could be attempted tomorrow. He nodded and dropped his hand from Bertie's face. "So," he said in a brighter tone in an attempt to clear the mood, "what is the first step in our project?"

Bertie grinned and picked up a paper with one hand—Pip was still clasping the other one. "Well, I thought we might run a few tests on the quizzing glass. I want to know how it reacts to different types of magic. I thought if I conduct the spells, you could see if you sense anything from it. You really have surpassed me in that field, you know."

Pip didn't attempt any false modesty. After months and months of training, he had developed a keen sense for magic. And having come by the skill naturally, learning how to control it made it even stronger. "I think that will do admirably." He turned a bit so he could look down at the paper in Bertie's hand. If he were honest with himself, he'd admit that he was stalling to avoid breaking up the current seating arrangement. He had a suspicion that Bertie wasn't opposed to the tactic. "Are these the tests?"

"Yes." Bertie tilted the paper so Pip could see it better. "I'm curious to know if it absorbs magic or deflects it. So I thought I'd try some simple basic spells on it first. I've charted out some things we can try, depending on the results of the first part."

"Do you have any predictions as to what it will do?"

Bertie smiled as if he knew what Pip was doing. Then he laid the paper down and leaned back in his seat, thus proving that he knew and was of the same mind. "Not really, I'm afraid."

"However did you come by it?"

Bertie chuckled and sat forward to open a large box on his desk. He pulled out the gold quizzing glass attached to a long gold chain, set it on the desk, and then leaned back in his seat again. "Bought it when I was traveling the continent with Charlie. We went on the Grand Tour together, you know. I found it in a charming little shop in Florence. Apparently, the shop owner had no idea what he had. I paid him triple what he was asking for it and considered myself lucky. Then again, I had no idea what he had either. But I knew it was of value."

Pip tentatively pushed the gold chain about on the desk surface. Bertie so rarely spoke about his past. While Pip could not blame him, as he hated speaking of his own past himself, he was very intrigued. "What exactly constitutes the Grand Tour? I don't know that you've ever talked about it."

Bertie gave a delicate shrug. "It is part of a firstborn's classic education. One is meant to understand culture and history and see the world."

"Where did you go?"

"Now let me see," Bertie said thoughtfully. He tapped his thumb against Pip's hand—a little tentatively, Pip thought.

Pip smiled and placed his other hand on Bertie's wrist in an effort to encourage it.

Bertie's small smile was the only acknowledgement of the gesture. "We started in Calais. Then went on to Paris, Geneva, Turin, Milan, Florence, Venice, Rome, Naples, Vienna, and then I think we returned home after that."

Pip felt a mix of emotions at this recitation. On the one hand, it awed him to think of visiting so many places and he wondered if he might convince Bertie to tell him stories of his travels. On the other hand, it put into stark relief how very different their upbringings had been. Bertie really was impossibly far above his own station.

Bertie went on, his expression thoughtful. "Of course, you

understand, these sorts of things usually last years. We were in Paris for a long time, you know."

"Yes, I understand. I should very much like to hear as much as you're willing to tell me."

Bertie gave his hand a gentle squeeze. "I'll tell you anything you like, dearest. And I must say, I've been thinking about making the trip again. Oh, not the whole of it, of course. I'm not sure I could handle it now. But perhaps a few cities. What do you think?"

"What do I think?"

"Yes, m'dear. What do you think of the notion of traveling together?"

Pip felt his eyes grow wide and his breath caught in his chest. "Bertie, do you—do you mean it?"

Bertie blinked at him. "Why, certainly."

"I think I should like that very much," Pip said softly.

"Wonderful. I hoped you might." He clapped his other hand on top of Pip's. "Now, would you like to begin our project?"

Pip exhaled and nodded. He released Bertie's hand and hopped down from the desk.

Together, they set up the study for spellcasting, moving furniture to the side and rolling back the carpet. Bertie had set out a collection of ingredients for spellcasting. He looked at them pensively.

"Hm. I rather think...yes. I think this will do to start. Would you be so kind as to fetch the quizzing glass, dear?"

Pip did and set it down on the floor where Bertie indicated. Then he stood back and watched as Bertie set up the spell. Bertie did not use spell bags; he was an advanced spellcaster and did not need them. He carefully measured out ingredients and set them around the glass. Pip began sensing to ensure everything was balanced properly. As Bertie was such an expert at magic, the spell was perfectly balanced.

"Ready?"

Pip nodded, focused.

Bertie murmured the incantation and the spell took hold. It was a simple spell, one for lateral movement with chalked lines within a large circle to indicate where the quizzing glass should move. The quizzing glass moved and Pip concentrated on how the glass reacted to the magic.

Bertie looked up. "Anything?"

Pip frowned. "Nothing unusual," he said slowly. The glass had simply moved around the circle; it hadn't glowed, sparkled, twirled, floated, or anything that he might have expected a magical item to do.

"Not entirely a bad thing. I'll try a couple more times just in case and then we'll move on to another spell."

He did as promised, and by the third time, Pip doubted himself enough to ask Bertie to swap positions.

He was relieved when Bertie shook his head. "You're quite right. Nothing out of the ordinary."

They cleaned up the spell and set up another one. This time, Bertie tried a levitation spell. But like the previous spell, it garnered the same results: nothing unusual happened to the quizzing glass, aside from being levitated. They cleaned up again and then Bertie suggested they take a break until after lunch.

"You see?" he said as he led Pip into the dining room. "I'm perfectly responsible when other people are around."

Pip raised an eyebrow. "That's only because you're more worried about other people than you are about yourself."

"A personality flaw I accept with good grace," Bertie said cheerily.

They ate lunch and chatted about their findings—or lack thereof—and what they meant. Pip was feeling a little discouraged and said as much.

"It isn't necessarily a bad thing," Bertie reminded him. "Perhaps it absorbs magic or deflects it."

"But then the spell should have been weaker or the magic should have moved outward or something." Pip paused. "How do you know the glass is a magical tool?"

Bertie chuckled. "I'll show you."

After they finished lunch, Bertie picked up the quizzing glass and held it up for Pip to see. "Do you see here?" he said, pointing with the tip of his little finger to the outside rim of the glass. "That little mark?"

Pip frowned and leaned closer to get a better view.

"That is the signature of Rodolfo Sandellini. He was a very important and influential magical theorist."

Pip bit his lip. "Is it not possible that it just happened to be... an ordinary quizzing glass that belonged to him?"

Bertie laughed, unoffended. "I suppose it is possible, but I believe that to be unlikely. Sandellini was an avid experimenter and most of his previous belongings have been bespelled somehow or other. He was a genius, really. But many of his writings and research were lost in a fire. So there's no knowing what information we are missing."

Pip traced the signature with his fingertip, thoughtful.

"Ready to try another?"

They began the process all over again, working steadily for hours until Bertie called for a break so they could sit down to tea. Pip was grateful that his visits were, at the very least, ensuring Bertie took care of himself. He resolved privately to make sure he arrived before lunch every day until Gerry came back.

By dinner they were both exhausted and nowhere nearer to solving the mystery.

"Don't lose heart, m'dear," Bertie said. "I still have a list of things I'd like to try."

After dinner, they retired to the sitting room and their favorite sofa. Pip leaned his head against Bertie's shoulder and picked up Bertie's hand to hold it in his lap. He had seen Laurence doing the same with Seb and thought it a sweet gesture. Bertie seemed inclined to agree, if the way the gentleman relaxed beneath him was anything to go by. They sat in comfortable silence together for a while.

After some time, Bertie said softly, "I hesitate to say anything for fear of discouraging, my darling, but I hope these additional signs of affection are not done out of anxiety for my sake."

Pip smiled even though Bertie couldn't see it. "No, they aren't. I am...exploring. If I do something that makes me uncomfortable, I won't repeat it...at least, not for a while."

"Very good, my sweet. As long as you're comfortable."

Pip picked up their clasped hands and kissed the inside of Bertie's wrist—something he'd seen Charles do with Gavin. Bertie tensed slightly in a way that suggested he was holding his breath.

"I'm always comfortable with you, Bertie." Pip said as he brought their hands back down to his lap and gave Bertie's a squeeze.

Bertie let out a long breath. "I'm glad to hear it, m'dear."

Pip sat up and looked at him. "I'm not making you uncomfortable, am I?"

"Oh, decidedly not."

Pip cocked his head. "But?"

Bertie huffed. "Well, I suppose I might as well tell you that I'm not entirely unaffected by your attention."

"I don't mean to tease you."

"Not a bit of it. Truly."

"Bertie..."

"Truly," Bertie repeated. "I am not feeling teased or frustrated, darling. Quite the opposite, actually. These little moments of affection...of-of trust...they mean more to me than I can possibly put into words. I'm a trifle..." He waved his hand as if seeking the right word. "Overcome by it. In a good way," he added hastily. "I'm adoring every second of it."

Pip studied his friend's face for a moment before relaxing back to lean on his shoulder. "You will tell me if I do anything untoward."

"Of course."

Pip chuckled. "Oh, Bertie. You know you won't."

Bertie squeezed his hand. "Only because I know you won't do anything I dislike."

"How can you be sure of that? I was with a man for years who did things I disliked, only I didn't tell him."

"Oh, good heavens, my sweet. Please be so kind as to never compare yourself to that monster ever again."

Pip smiled. "I suppose it is different with us."

"Most decidedly different."

Pip lifted their hands again to kiss Bertie's wrist once more.

Bertie sighed and Pip was relieved to note that it was definitely a happy sort of sigh.

When he got home, he found Charles and Gavin sitting exactly where they had been the previous night. Only this time, Gavin had fallen asleep with the book on his lap, and Charles was idly stroking through his husband's hair.

"Good evening, darling," he said quietly when Pip walked in. "Did you have a good visit?"

"Yes. We're working on a project. A sort of magical experiment. More exhausting than I would have expected."

Charles smiled. "I imagine Bertie is having the time of his life, though."

Pip returned the smile. "Yes, I think he is."

"About the conversation we had this morning: I do hope you know you can talk to me about anything."

Pip perched on the edge of a chair. "I will probably take you up on that," he said slowly. "But not yet, I think. Perhaps later this week, I can go riding with you in the morning. Would that suit?"

"That would suit admirably. I get up at the same time each day. Tell your valet the evening before and he'll see to it you're woken up when I am."

"Thank you, Charles." He got up to leave the room and then turned, suddenly. "I think you should know," he started. Then he hesitated.

Charles looked up at him expectantly. "Yes, darling?"

"You and Gavin...it was living with you two that made me understand what love could be like. I'd...I'd never seen a love like yours before."

Charles gave him a wide, dazzling smile.

"I thought I ought to tell you."

"And I hope *you* know, dearest, that you are loved. Oh, not just in the way we're talking now. But, by me and Gavin, Gerry, Seb. Julian. I'm sure I don't tell you often enough how much you mean to us."

Pip felt as though he might cry. He gave a brusque nod. "Thank you."

"It pleases me more than I can say," Charles went on. "To think that you will always be in our lives...in some way or another."

Trust Charles to bring it up like that.

"Yes, well. That's yet to be determined, isn't it?"

"Is it?" Charles said, his smile sly.

Pip rolled his eyes. "Good night, Charles."

DAY THREE

The next morning, breakfast was a far quieter affair. Seb practically inhaled his food—which earned him a mild scolding from his brother—and then left to spend time with his betrothed.

Charles chuckled at the young man's alacrity. "Oh dear. I suppose we are quickly losing our appeal."

Gavin rolled his eyes. "It's Seb. Are you surprised?"

Pip glanced uncertainly between them. "Will you two be all right when he moves out? I don't like the idea of you being lonely."

Charles grinned. "Not a bit of it. We adore having you all here, but I will be pleased as anything when you and Seb are as happily settled as Gerry."

"My sentiments are the same," Gavin assured him. "Even if I'm not so blunt about it as Charles."

Charles smiled and leaned forward to rub Gavin's cheek affectionately. Gavin, as usual, blushed, although he no longer seemed to mind the displays of affection like he used to.

Pip bid his farewells and left for Bertie's, thinking about that change. He was not fond of public displays of affection; he never had been. His previous lover, the one Bertie hated discussing, had frequently been publicly affectionate, using Pip's distaste for it as a punishment. He knew Gavin's lack of fondness was rooted more in shyness and modesty. But it did make Pip wonder if his tastes might evolve over time as well.

As he walked toward Bertie's house, he pondered the matter. Most of the time, he felt affection to be incredibly intimate and showing it in front of others was horrifying. But he could imagine himself becoming gradually more comfortable in their own small social circle. He was a little struck by the revelation. The friends he had made in Tutting-on-Cress, this family of sorts, had made him feel safer than he had ever thought possible. It was remarkable to realize that his trust in them could continue to grow. He mulled over the feeling as he walked, and decided he liked it.

He was so caught up in his thoughts that the rain took him completely by surprise. It was not a torrential downpour, just a steady drizzle. He picked up the pace, but he was such a considerable distance from Bertie's when it started that he was thoroughly soaked when he arrived. As such, he asked the footman to tell Bertie he had arrived and waited in the foyer to avoid tracking water and mud all over the house.

Bertie hurried out to greet him. "Good heavens, darling. You're soaked to the skin."

"I am sorry. I didn't think to look about me. I'm not usually so absent-minded."

"You sweet thing, there's no need for apologies. Let's get you out of these wet clothes now. Come along." Bertie placed a gentle hand behind Pip's back and led him up the stairs.

Pip was a little surprised when he was led into Bertie's bedroom. He felt himself flush at the intimacy of it, although he looked around the large room with interest.

Poor Bertie was clearly flustered by the sight of Pip in a

bedraggled state. He ordered a bath to be drawn, even though Pip assured him it was unnecessary, and sent for a pot of tea. He draped a banyan made of quilted burgundy velvet over the edge of the bed. "I'll have someone perform a drying spell on your clothes immediately, but this might help to keep you warm in the meantime."

Pip was a little embarrassed to be made such a fuss over, and he was quite certain that the drying spells would dry his clothes instantaneously, but he could see that his friend was genuinely concerned, so he didn't argue.

Bertie left the room as soon as his valet started undressing Pip.

He really didn't need the bath, so he sat it in long enough to feel warmed by it, and then got up to be dried. The clothes had been taken away to be cleaned as well as dried, so he slid into the banyan. It was far too big for him as Bertie was both taller and rounder. But it smelled like Bertie and was deliciously comfortable. Pip tied the belt tightly around his waist. He decided this would have to be his bold move for the day as he had certainly missed the opportunity to ruffle Bertie's hair. He asked timidly if the tea could be brought down to the sitting room instead and went downstairs to find Bertie.

Bertie was pacing at the bottom of the stairs. "Oh goodness, darling. You didn't need to rush. You couldn't have possibly enjoyed your bath at that rate."

Pip smiled and reached out his hand. "But I came here to visit you. I would much prefer to be in your company than in the bath."

Bertie took his hand. "You sweet thing." He fussed a bit at the banyan, making sure it was wrapping about Pip fully. Then he seemed to realize what he was doing and stopped. "Good heavens," he murmured. "I'm so sorry, my sweet."

Pip squeezed his hand. "I don't mind it. Although I don't like to see you worried."

Bertie gave him a small smile. "Let's get you to the fire so you don't catch a chill. Did you have the tea?"

"I asked for it to be sent downstairs instead. I hope that was all right."

"But of course, m'dear. Of course." He got Pip situated on the sofa closest to the fire, propping pillows behind him as if he were an invalid.

Pip laughed. "I truly am fine, Bertie. Just got a bit wet, that's all."

Bertie nodded and sank down on the sofa beside him. Pip took Bertie's hand in both of his and leaned against his shoulder as they waited for the tea to be brought in.

"I must confess," Bertie said as he poured out. "I quite like that color on you. Very becoming."

"Is it?" Pip said, pleased, as he sat up.

"You look perfectly adorable in it."

"I quite like it. Very comfortable."

"If it were a better fit for you, I'd make a gift of it."

Pip gave him a sidelong glance. "Well, truth be told, Bertie, I like it so much because it's rather exciting wearing something of yours. You don't mind, do you?"

Bertie blushed. "Goodness me, no. I might add that you wearing it is adding significantly to the garment's appeal."

Pip laughed and accepted the teacup. He sipped at his tea, looking at Bertie over the rim. It had been a while since Bertie had flirted with him. The first time they met, the gentleman had proved to be an outrageous flirt, but ever since Bertie had encountered Pip's former lover, he had been careful to avoid such things. Pip was incredibly grateful for his friend's thoughtfulness, but he had also never really minded Bertie's particular brand of flirting.

"You're looking at me very pensively over that teacup," Bertie remarked. "Anything on your mind?"

Pip smiled. "Yes. I was just thinking how long it had been since you flirted with me, and I quite like that you're beginning to do it again."

Bertie chuckled. "I'm attempting to follow your lead, darling. I hope that's all right?"

"Most assuredly. As a matter of fact..." He hesitated.

Bertie waited, patient.

Pip set his cup down. "We never really talk about these things because, well, it's hard to talk about it...I love that you are so careful about touching me. As I know you're aware, my..." He paused. "Well, let's say rather, *he* touched me often and it made me feel as though my body was never truly my own."

"Darling," Bertie said softly.

Pip reached out and took his hand. "It has been a glorious time living here and knowing that no one has that sort of claim on me. And furthermore..." He took a breath. "Well, I wasn't sure when I'd be ready for love...again. Or for...touch again." He huffed. "Or for intimacy. There were times when I wasn't sure I'd ever be ready for such a thing."

"I hope you know that it would never be an expectation," Bertie said. "Not in my case, at least. Your good company is enough."

Pip smiled at him fondly. "I know." He let out a shaky laugh. "There are things I want to tell you, but it is difficult to get the words out."

Bertie set his teacup aside and put his other hand around Pip's. "Take your time, darling. And know that you do not have to say anything, if it makes you uncomfortable."

"After our meeting at the Fox & Thistle..." He carefully did not look at Bertie as he said that. "Well, it was a particularly horrid time for me. Nell was gone. And though she wasn't really a buffer of any sort, she was still comforting to be around. But then she left. And I felt so stuck, knowing that she had gone to live with you and that I might have come too, only I couldn't. And Jack...he was even worse. Now that I know better, I can see that he was trying to tighten his hold on me. Going to prison was practically a relief, although I can't deny I was frightened." He closed his eyes and said, "But in the nights that followed our meeting, when I had no friends and no hope, when it was just me and Jack..." He looked down at his lap. "I would close my eyes and imagine it was you instead. Even when you weren't around and I thought I'd never see you again, the very thought of you was an escape for me. I've never told you that because it felt so...foolish and impossible. But..." He looked up. "Bertie, I don't know when I'll be ready for that sort of thing again, but I do know I want it. Because I know that with you it will be different. Just like everything with you has been different."

Bertie looked like he might cry. "Oh, petal," he said softly.

Pip smiled and reached up to cup Bertie's cheek, as he had the previous day. "I say all of this...well, I want you to know that it is something I've thought about. That I still think about. And, I am so impossibly grateful you have given me the space to indicate when I'm comfortable with things. But..." He took a deep breath. "Well, I'm trying to be bolder. I want...I want to be bolder. But I'm so frightened by it. Do you think you could... help?"

Bertie beamed at him. "Gladly, my darling. Will you promise to tell me if I do anything you do not like?"

"If you'll promise the same."

Bertie reached up to cover the hand on his cheek. He rubbed Pip's knuckles gently with his thumb. "I promise." Then, still covering Pip's hand to keep it in place, Bertie turned his head slightly and pressed a soft kiss to Pip's palm. Clasping Pip's hand, he brought both down to where their other hands were still together.

"Thank you, Bertie." He folded himself forward to lean his head against Bertie's shoulder.

Bertie stroked his back gently with one hand and they sat together in the quiet until the footman came in and informed Bertie that Pip's clothes had been cleaned, dried, and pressed and placed back upstairs.

Pip sat up. "I'd better go change."

Bertie smiled and gave the lapel a light stroke. "I suppose we'll have to find another excuse to have you wear this again, won't we?"

Pip laughed and kissed Bertie's cheek before getting up and following the footman back to the bedroom. As nervous and tongue-tied as he had felt confessing all of that to Bertie, he felt lighter than he had in ages.

"So," Pip said as he walked back into the sitting room in his own clothes, "now that we have intimate confessions and fears out of the way, shall we continue with our project?"

Bertie chuckled. "I was actually going to suggest eating lunch first. Do you mind?"

Pip shook his head and sat back down on the sofa. "Not at all. We can discuss your plans for the next part while we wait."

Bertie nodded and immediately took Pip's hand in his own. Pip felt as though his heart would burst at the gesture. "More of the same, I'm afraid. Although this time, I want to try Motion spells to see if that has any significant impact."

They ate a leisurely lunch before going to the study for more experimentation. Bertie requested that a fire be built in the study. He claimed it was because the rainy weather made him yearn for coziness, but Pip suspected Bertie was still concerned about him. They took turns performing Motion spells on the quizzing glass and sensing to see if it reacted in any sort of unusual way. It didn't. Pip forbore repeating his suspicions that the quizzing glass might actually be a simple quizzing glass.

Because the Motion spells required no set up and fewer ingredients, they went through Bertie's list a great deal faster than they had the previous day. By the time they stopped for another pot of tea, they had completed his list. After tea, Bertie performed different sorts of magical experiments on the quizzing glass. He explained what he was doing very carefully and clearly, but Pip had never had much patience for theory, so he contented himself with observing and assisting when he could.

He watched as Bertie made calculations and then used magical tools and ingredients on the glass. Some of the spells Bertie cast looked deceptively simple but were, Bertie explained, a great deal more dangerous and powerful. At times, he didn't use chalk at all, but employed different fine powders or liquids to draw circles and sigils around the quizzing glass. Tiny explosions popped in the air above the glass or vibrated the floorboards. But still, the quizzing glass refused to do anything remotely interesting. It floated when directed to float, slid when directed to slide, spun when directed to spin, and so on.

By dinner, Pip was so discouraged, he felt as tired as he had the previous day, even though he had done considerably less work.

When he said as much to Bertie, the other man said, "M'dear, you underestimate what a challenging day it's been, even before we started our project."

Pip inclined his head in agreement.

After dinner, they retired back to the sitting room. Pip nestled close to Bertie and relished the way Bertie wrapped his arm gently around him.

Emboldened by the port he was drinking and his earlier

confessions, Pip surprised himself by asking, "Can I ask you something I've wondered for years now?"

"You can ask me anything you like."

"Why do you and Charles always use terms of endearment? When I first met you both, I thought it was an upper-class thing. But none of the Hartfords do it, nor do the Thornes, nor the Ladies Windham—well, Lady Caro does, I suppose—but you know what I mean."

Bertie chuckled and took a sip of port before answering. "At this point, it is more a matter of habit and our naturally affectionate natures. But it was a habit years in the making. We practically grew up together, you know, Charlie and I. Our mothers were very close. We were like brothers, really. We did everything together. And when we were sent away to school, we were sent to the same ones. That's where it started, you see. We were both very excited about meeting new people and hopeful of meeting potential beaux. But we learned very quickly that most people weren't quite as interested in knowing us."

"Really? That surprises me."

"Well, perhaps I should clarify that I mean no one wanted to really *know* us. There were plenty of people clamoring to become acquaintances and plenty more claiming friendship, but precious few who could look past the wealth and the status. So, we developed a code. We had always had a sort of easy affection around each other, so we started calling each other all sorts of things like 'darling' and 'dear' and 'sweetling.' And we did it so often that soon no one else thought it strange that we should do it. Then we would use the terms of endearment on people who we deemed to be genuine friends. So, if Charlie brought around a fellow and said, 'Darling, allow me to introduce Bertie Finlington,' I would know that he thought the fellow to be a good sort."

"I always thought you used it on everybody."

Bertie laughed. "That is because we are blessedly surrounded by decent people."

Pip considered for a moment. "Didn't you call Nell and I such things when we first met?"

"I seem to recall I did," Bertie said, a smile in his voice.

"You thought *we* were a good sort? When we were robbing your house?"

"As I've pointed out before, m'dear, neither of you were greedy enough to steal anything besides what you were sent for. I saw that before I even saw you. I could tell right away that you weren't ordinary burglars and that you were after something particular. And most people who are after something particular are working on behalf of someone else. I've never encountered a thief who didn't take advantage of the opportunity to pocket something valuable for themselves. Until you two. I was intrigued to say the least."

Pip pondered this. "I thought you two might be together when I first met you."

Bertie chuckled. "You wouldn't be the first. Our tendencies towards endearments doesn't help. I rather think our mothers expected us to fall in love. Actually, I rather think they hoped we would. Particularly when we both showed attraction for the masculine earlier on. Well," he added, "Charlie has always been of both persuasions."

"I don't think I knew that," Pip said.

"Didn't you? Well, he is rather private about it, so I suppose that shouldn't surprise me."

"Odd to think of Charles being private about anything."

Bertie laughed aloud at that.

"He won't mind, will he? That I know?" Pip asked. "Not that I'll mention it or anything."

"You sweet thing," Bertie said. "No, he won't mind. He

doesn't dislike people knowing. He simply doesn't talk about it often. If you ask me, he used to be that way because he liked being mysterious."

Pip tilted his head back a little to look at Bertie. "Charles? Mysterious?"

"Oh yes, he was quite the popular figure when we first entered London society. Nobody knew his persuasion, you see. And he was so dashed charming to everyone that he kept people guessing. Every time a rumor would circulate that he was of the masculine persuasion, another would crop up shortly after that he was of the feminine persuasion." Bertie chortled. "It was most entertaining. And of course, everyone was trying to catch his eye because he was so wealthy and handsome. We both made considerable use of our code then, too. It became vitally important in protecting each other from fortune hunters and other such leeches."

Pip felt a little worried for a moment. Would he be considered a fortune hunter, being so below Bertie's station?

Bertie took a sip of port and continued. "And then of course Charlie met dear Gavin, who liked him for himself. So that was all right."

Pip let out a breath of relief, feeling silly for the momentary fear. "I suppose I should ask them. But I don't know the story of how they met."

Bertie gave a little huff of amusement, as if to himself. "Yes, I think you should ask them. It's quite a romantic story. Although I should warn you that they will likely each tell you something a little different."

Pip wondered at this.

"I can tell you, however, that Charlie was quite smitten almost immediately. I remember the day he came to my house to tell me he'd finally managed an introduction. He spoke of Gavin in such rapturous tones that I had to invite the sweet man to the very next dinner party I held. He barely spoke a word to anyone all evening. It was the most adorable thing." Bertie sighed. "I confess I teased the poor fellow throughout their courtship. He always gave the most endearing reactions."

"I suppose that I should take it as a matter of course that Charles now teases me," Pip said with a smile.

"Does he, the rascal?" Bertie said without rancor. "Yes, I daresay you should. It means he gives his blessing, you know."

Pip felt warmed by the words. "Yes," he murmured. "I hoped as much."

He set his glass of port aside and snuggled closer, enjoying the comforting closeness. He felt Bertie tentatively stroke his arm with the backs of his fingers. The rain pattered gently outside the window. The fire was delightfully cozy. Pip closed his eyes contentedly and fell asleep.

HE WOKE up to see the fire burning low and felt groggily confused and comfy. But when he realized where he was and why he was so comfy, he sprang up in alarm.

"Oh, good heavens, Bertie! Why didn't you wake me?"

Bertie looked nonplussed. "Why on earth would I do that, darling?"

"I don't even know what time it is."

"A little past two, I think," Bertie said in a musing sort of tone.

"You let me sleep like that until two in the morning?" Pip asked, aghast.

"How could I possibly wake you when you looked so sweet curled up against me?" Bertie said, giving Pip's cheek a swift and gentle stroke with his thumb.

Pip huffed, part from amusement and part from embarrassment. "You didn't mind?"

"Mind? Far from it."

Pip gave him a small smile. "You mean to say you liked it?"

Bertie leaned forward. "I adored it. I quite like the idea of more evenings spent like that."

Pip's smile widened. "So do I," he said quietly. "I've thought that, actually, when I've seen the way Charles and Gavin—" He broke off. "Oh, goodness. They'll be so worried. I'd better get home."

Bertie held up a hand. "I sent a note hours ago to tell them you were safe and would be late getting back."

Pip breathed a sigh of relief. "Good. Thank you." He stood up and got his bearings a little. It was strange seeing the room in the dark of early morning. It made him feel as if the most natural thing in the world would be to head upstairs for bed. He was not ready for that line of thought so he swiftly cast about for something else. He ran a hand through his hair, distracted and unsure. "I suppose I ought to go home."

"Probably best, my sweet. I'll send for the carriage."

Pip paced the room, trying to wake up a little more. He felt a mixture of emotions: he was keenly embarrassed, but there was also a small thrill of pleasure that he had done something so domestic as fall asleep on Bertie's shoulder—and that Bertie had liked it.

Bertie walked back into the room, having sent someone to bring around the carriage. "Are you all right, m'dear?"

Pip wasn't entirely sure he should say what was on his mind, but he was too sleepy to be sharp, so he said nothing.

Bertie stepped in front of him, halting his pacing. "You're not regretting it, I hope? Staying so late, I mean."

"Not exactly," Pip said. "Only..."

"Yes, dear?"

"Was it...wrong? Of me? Of us?"

Bertie gave him a small smile. "By whose standards?"

"I'm not sure," Pip said. "I mean to say, you're a gentleman and everything. I'm not tarnishing your...your reputation. Am I?"

Bertie chuckled. "If either of us were a nextborn, there might be some cause for concern. If my intentions weren't entirely honorable, then I daresay we could be courting scandal. And if we didn't live in a tiny area where the only people who will know of this are Charlie and Gavin—at worst, Seb will learn of it and tell Laury—then I might be worried for *your* reputation. I'm certainly not worried about mine," he added blithely. "But Charlie knows us both well enough to know that I would never treat you so shamefully. Gavin does as well. Even if Seb does get shocking ideas in his head, he's no gossip. And Laury is far too open-minded a person to care at all. So you're perfectly safe."

"I am more worried about you than myself. Goodness knows, with my history...but this is also the first time I've done anything like this in my current station."

Bertie held out his hand and Pip slid his into it. "Please don't fret. I can assure you neither of us will suffer any social repercussions. Unless you count the fact that Charlie will most definitely tease us both."

Pip grinned at the thought. "Won't he ever."

Bertie squeezed his hand and led him out of the room. "Let's get you to bed now, darling."

Pip let the footman help him into his things, then leaned forward and kissed Bertie's cheek. "Thank you, Bertie," he said. "I had a marvelous time."

Bertie smiled. "A pleasure as always, my sweet."

Bertie turned out to be right, of course. Charles did tease

him. He was waiting up, sitting in the front drawing room so as to have a clear view of when Pip walked in the door.

"Have a good time, darling?" he asked in a singsong voice.

Pip chuckled and walked into the room. He leaned against the doorjamb. "Oh, yes. I always do, you know."

"I'm delighted to hear it," Charles said with a grin. "Will I have the pleasure of your company tomorrow for my morning ride?"

Pip scoffed. "After staying up this late?"

"Oh, but darling, I am simply consumed with curiosity."

"I do apologize. I'm very much afraid you will have to be consumed for a little while longer."

Charles laughed as he stood. "Well, I might as well enjoy it while it lasts." He tucked his hand under Pip's elbow and began walking him up the stairs. "After you, whose business will I have left to poke my nose into?"

Pip grinned. "Some of the Thorne children are getting close to the right age, I should think."

"Ah, how right you are! Thank you, dearest. You've certainly put my mind at rest."

DAY FOUR

"—And then we're going to dig trenches across the space for better irrigation, and Laury is going to cast a spell to keep the water moving when needed. Of course, it will have to be carefully observed to ensure it doesn't cause root rot or any sort of oversaturation of the soil. The trick will be to install a tool to gauge moisture levels and Laury's plan is to put together something like a weather cock..."

To Pip's relief, no one said a word at breakfast about his late night. He noticed that Gavin's mouth twitched a little—a sign that the young man was trying not to smile—but Gavin had never been one to tease Pip much.

Seb seemed completely oblivious to the whole thing, as all he wanted to discuss was the progress he and Laurence were making on the garden expansion. No one else in the household knew anything whatsoever about gardening or planting. With Gerry moved out, there wasn't even a person left with an academic interest in magical plant life. So the conversation was mostly Seb talking a great deal about the project, and everyone else offering encouragement and expressions of "How interesting!" when the timing seemed right. Pip was intrigued when

Seb explained that Laurence had constructed a sort of temporary tent for them to work under during the rain. But other than that tidbit, everything went completely over his head. He felt a little guilty about it, but Seb didn't seem to mind. After he ran out of details to report, he left.

"I wish I knew more about gardening," Pip said.

Gavin gave a brief huff of laughter. "You think he knows in the least what he's talking about?"

Pip grinned.

"I must say I'll miss his chatter when he's married and gone," Charles said fondly.

Gavin nodded, looking grave. Gavin always looked grave, but he looked especially thoughtful in his gravity.

Charles smiled at his husband. "Before we know it, it will be just us two old married men left, darling."

Pip thought he saw a flicker of worry in Gavin's expression. But Gavin's tone was light when he said, "Speak for yourself. I'm five years younger than you."

Charles laughed and leaned forward to stroke Gavin's cheek. "You know there isn't anyone I'd rather spend the rest of my days with," he said in a soft voice. Then he cupped Gavin's chin and pulled him in for a brief kiss.

Gavin was blushing furiously and he cleared his throat as soon as the kiss ended. "I do beg your pardon, Pip."

Pip smiled. "I don't mind. I was just telling Charles the other day how you two taught me what love ought to look like."

Gavin looked down, self-conscious. "Charles is the real role model there, I'm afraid. He's easy to love. I'm—"

"Perfect," Charles said in a tone that brooked no argument.

Gavin looked up at his husband adoringly.

In what was likely an effort to save Gavin from being the center of attention, Charles reached for his husband's hand and then pivoted his focus back to Pip. "And what time should we expect you home, darling?"

Pip resisted the urge to roll his eyes. "I don't think I'll make that mistake again. Don't worry."

"Whyever not?" Charles said. "I think it's adorably romantic, personally."

"Oh, do stop teasing him," Gavin said.

A footman stepped up to the table and held a note on a silver tray to Pip.

Pip picked it up, confused, and then recognized the handwriting. "It's from Bertie."

"Go ahead and read it at the table if you'd like, darling," Charles said. "You know we don't stand on ceremony here."

Pip was confident Charles really just wanted to know what the letter said, but he didn't mind.

DARLING,

Laury has asked me to come look at his garden expansion and offer advice. I hope you will not be disappointed when I admit that I accepted his invitation. If you would care to accompany me, I can collect you on my way. Otherwise, I would be more than happy to pick you up on my way back.

Affectionately,

Bertie

PIP FOLDED THE NOTE, and because Charles was looking at him expectantly (Gavin had politely returned his attention to his food), he said, "He's going to Copperage Farm to give Laurence advice on the garden project. Invited me to come along." He smiled guiltily. "Would it be awful of me to tell him I'd rather meet him on the way back? I'm not sure I could pretend knowledge of such things a second time in one morning."

"God, no," Gavin said. "I'm sure I couldn't."

"Why don't you invite him to stay for lunch on his return trip?" Charles said.

Pip agreed and went to the library to write his reply. After he sent the message off, he strolled back to the breakfast room, a little unsure of what to do with himself until lunch.

Gavin and Charles were still sitting where he'd left them, and none of the breakfast things had been cleared away yet. So Pip sat back down to finish his meal. Gavin poured him another cup of tea.

"So, what to do with the free morning, my dear?" Charles said.

Pip smiled into his teacup. "Oh, very well. We'll have our ride as soon as I'm done eating. But you must know, my thoughts are still terribly jumbled. So it is highly likely I will make no sense whatsoever."

"Delightful."

Gavin rolled his eyes. "Oh, really. You are incorrigible. Do you know?"

Charles grinned, completely unrepentant and lifted Gavin's hand to kiss his inner wrist, which aptly put a stop to Gavin's protestations on Pip's behalf.

After breakfast, Pip followed Charles to the stables and they rode out across lush countryside. Charles, to his credit, did not start the conversation right away. He led them both on a canter for a good quarter hour before slowing his horse to a trot. Pip was grateful for it, as it allowed him to work off his nerves and try to figure out what he might say.

When Charles looked at him expectantly, he started with, "We had a good long talk yesterday."

"Oh yes?"

"You see, I've been trying to be a bit bolder. You know he never touches me unless I initiate the contact?"

Charles nodded.

"Well, as I've said, I've been trying to work up the courage for more...signs of affection. It hasn't been much," he added a little hastily. "I touched his cheek. A-and kissed his cheek. Laid our hands in my lap. And kissed the inside of his wrist, you know, like..." He glanced at Charles.

Charles grinned. "It all sounds wonderfully romantic, darling. Do go on."

Thus encouraged, Pip said, "I told him yesterday that I'm still working on it. On being bold, I mean. And I told him that as much as I appreciate him not touching me, I think it has been a bit too much for it to all fall on me to push things along. So I asked him to help."

"I take it he agreed?"

Pip nodded. "We're both so tentative about it. But I'm relieved it isn't just me reaching out now."

"I can imagine."

Pip took a deep breath. "What's troubling me now is that I'm not sure what comes next. I mean...well...I'm quite fond of him, Charles," he said on an exhale. "In fact, I love him. And I'm tolerably certain he feels the same—"

"Oh, I can assure you he does," Charles said, beaming.

"So, what do I do now? Do I..." He couldn't bring himself to say it. He took another steadying breath. "I expect he will be just as careful to not...ask me to marry him," saying the last few words in a rush, "because he won't want me to feel hurried or pressured. So...am I meant to do it?"

"I'm very much afraid you might have to be the one," Charles said, his smile sympathetic. "I'd offer to talk to him for you—"

"Oh, heavens, please don't."

"—but I imagine he won't listen to me," Charles finished with a laugh. "He is fiercely protective of you. Well, we both are. No," he amended, "we all are."

Pip chuckled, feeling some of his tension dissipate. "I know."

"He won't ask you because, as you said, he'll be afraid of rushing you. He would wait for years for you."

"I know," Pip said quietly.

"What makes you hesitant to ask him?" Charles said, matching his tone.

Pip considered the question. "I'm not sure," he said at last. "I know long engagements are an option. Although I worry that would put me in precisely the same position, only delayed somewhat."

"More than likely," Charles agreed. "So is that your concern? You aren't ready?"

"I suppose. Only, I know that once we were married, he wouldn't rush me anymore than he does now. So I would have nothing to fear in terms of...intimacy. And..." Pip felt himself blush at his upcoming confession. "I do miss sharing a bed with someone. So I think I'd be ready for that, especially with Bertie. Even if we didn't do anything. I...I think it would be rather blissful." He glanced at Charles, who was looking at him fondly. So he kept going. "And I must confess, there is a part of me that is worried about proposing marriage when we haven't even kissed, and we're only just getting more comfortable with some level of affection, but I know marriages take some time to prepare, so we would have time to grow more comfortable."

"That is certainly true," Charles said. "And I should note, that if you two were engaging in a more official sort of courtship, you would be unlikely to have any more physical affection than you already have. Granted, you are both first-borns, or considered as such. The social rules of etiquette are a good deal gentler with firstborns than with nextborns. But it's more a matter of society looking away from what firstborns do, rather than there not being a rule at all. If that makes sense."

"It does. So, if we were in a typical sort of courtship, we wouldn't be expected to do more than hold hands or kiss each other's cheek?"

"If you were in a typical courtship, people would see you both as behaving very correctly. Well," he added with a sly grin, "late-night visits notwithstanding."

"Oh," Pip said, rolling his eyes. "You know perfectly well nothing happened."

Charles chuckled. "Technically, by rights, you ought to have a chaperone. But since this is not an official courtship and you're starting off as friends, those sorts of rules can be overlooked."

Having run out of all of his pent-up reasons for procrastinating, Pip took a shaky breath and nodded. "All right."

"All right?" Charles said, excitement in his tone.

"All right. I'll do it. I'm not sure when, but I'll do it."

Charles grinned broadly. "How marvelous, darling."

"So on the way back home, you can tell me the proper way of things."

"Can I?"

"Isn't there a proper way of things? I'm quite out of my depth here, you know. Do I—" he broke off, feeling a small frisson of panic. "Good heavens. I won't have to ask his parents, will I?"

Charles laughed. "No, darling. He's of age. You can simply ask him."

Pip let out a deep breath. "Oh, thank goodness."

Charles led them both toward home. "Now, as to the rest, there's no formal way of asking. Some people kneel to propose. That can be very romantic. Although, I didn't."

"How did you propose?"

"We were walking down the street. He had just told me he loved me. I wanted to kiss him in response, but Gavin is far too proper and shy to do such a thing in public, especially without a declaration. So I proposed right then and there."

"Were you nervous?"

Charles smiled at the memory. "I wasn't when I asked him the question. But for a while, I hadn't been sure of his interest. It was months of courting him and becoming his friend and trying to determine his persuasion, let alone determine if he cared for me the way I cared for him. Then we danced together at a ball, which cleared a great many of my doubts. Then he gave me a very fine gift. And when I kissed him, he kissed me back." Charles's smile broadened. "I was still unsure if he was ready for me to propose, until he sent me a letter and signed it 'Yours.'" He turned to Pip. "And then I knew. I dropped everything I was doing and left for London to propose to him immediately."

Pip smiled. "I suppose with Gavin it must have been difficult to know. He's very reserved."

"Very."

"So there's nothing particular I need to say?"

"Nothing exact, no. You know the sentiment already. As long as you get that across, you'll do just fine."

Pip nodded. They rode in silence for a while. "Oh," he said suddenly.

"What is it?"

"Will I have to do what Gavin does? Run the house?"

Charles smiled. "You'll be so very good at it, darling." He laughed at Pip's shocked expression. "Don't fret about it. Gavin will teach you everything you need to know before you move out. There's plenty of time. It isn't as if Bertie won't help you. You know the man would swim the Thames for you, don't you?"

Pip grinned. "He really is wonderful, isn't he?"

Charles's smile widened. "Oh, dearest. I cannot possibly tell you how happy it makes me to see Bertie loved so well at last. You both deserve each other."

Buoyed by this statement, Pip followed Charles home in high spirits.

As soon as they reached the house, Charles went to his study and Pip went to the library. The library was, for Pip, a rather odd sort of place. On the one hand, he always felt uniquely inferior standing in a room full of knowledge and information. He hadn't learned to read until he moved to Tutting-on-Cress, so the library was like a constant reminder of how little he really knew, how little education he received, and how humble his beginnings were. On the other hand, he had his own shelf in the library that Gerry had been diligent about keeping well stocked for him (he suspected Gavin of stocking it as well, when no one was looking). That little shelf had been one of the first things that made Pip feel truly at home in Tutting-on-Cress. While the library represented for him how much he lacked in terms of education and knowledge, it was also where he learned to read and first had the courage to talk about his troubles to his friends. Sometimes being there was like poking at a scab to see if it still smarted.

He paced the length of the library, turning the conversation with Charles over in his mind. He tried practicing the inevitable conversation with Bertie. But every time he started, he got flustered and had to start over. He was beginning to work himself into a tizzy and finally sat down at the library desk. He drummed his fingers against the desktop, trying to calm his nerves.

After some deliberation, he pulled fresh paper out of the drawer and onto the desk, and composed a letter to his friend

Nell Birks. The last he'd heard from her, she'd informed him that she wouldn't be able to make it to Gerry's wedding.

Dear Nell,

I'm glad you're still enjoying your new duties in training spellcasters. You always were good at taking people under your wing, so that sort of task seems perfect for you. How are your friends? Please give them my regards, and please assure Lino that I'm very happy in the country.

It is nice to hear that Patience is still doing well. I worry sometimes about how the others fared after Jack's arrest. But it sounds as though Patience, at least, is thriving. If her daughters are taking to learning as well as you say, then I imagine they have a bright future ahead of them.

As to the subject of me visiting London, I'm not sure when it will happen. But I was recently offered the opportunity to travel more. As much as I dislike London, I think a brief stay in the city could be quite nice, especially if it meant seeing you and the dukex.

So I hope to see you again soon.

Affectionately,

Pip

HE FOLDED THE LETTER, addressed it, and sat back in his chair. He and Nell did not correspond very often so he anticipated it taking a while to hear back from her.

With that task complete, he cast about for something else to focus on. What would Bertie want to do next with the quizzing glass? He frowned and looked around the library. Who was it Bertie said the glass belonged to? Perhaps knowing more about the fellow would give Pip a better idea of the sort of man he was, and what he might do with a quizzing glass. He remembered the name was of Italian extraction. He began to slowly walk along the walls of the library, hoping something would jog his memory.

Seb walked in before he'd gone past one wall.

"What ho!" Seb said cheerily.

"Back already?"

"We came back with Bertie for lunch. I was sent to look for you."

"Do you remember the names of any Italian magical theorists?"

Seb shrugged. "Sandellini is the only one I remember."

"I think that was it! What do you know about him?"

Seb puffed out his cheeks. "Not much. I only learned what I had to, you know, for my studies."

"I've never had much of a head for theory. What was it he wrote about?"

"He's the fellow who came up with the Constitutional Properties." Seb strolled confidently to one shelf in the library and looked at the books carefully. "You know, all that muck about everything having a personality and whatnot. Gerry made me memorize the list. It took ages." He pulled out a few books. "Here's the official list of Constitutional Properties," he said, handing one to Pip. "Here's more of Sandellini's theories and studies and rot. And this is his life and times, et cetera."

Pip took all the books eagerly. "Thank you!"

"What is it you're looking for?"

"I'm not sure, to be honest. Bertie and I are working on a project that has to do with him and I thought knowing more about him might help."

Pip put the stack of books on his own half-empty shelf so he could find them easily later. Then he followed Seb out of the library.

The others were in the sitting room, waiting for lunch.

Laurence had taken one seat on the sofa. Seb immediately made for the open seat. Gavin was sitting in the chair closest to Laurence, talking to him in his usual serious manner. Charles was perched on the arm of Gavin's chair, talking to Bertie, who was sitting in the chair beside him. There was an open seat next to Bertie and Pip suspected that Charles had pointedly left it available for him, so he took it.

Bertie smiled fondly at Pip when he took his seat, but did not reach a hand out to him. Pip guessed that the viscount was waiting for a cue from Pip to determine whether they were going to be affectionate in company. He was grateful for it. He wasn't sure he was ready for that yet.

"How was your visit?" Pip asked.

"It was marvelous, darling. Thank you. Laury has everything well set up, which is entirely unsurprising."

"He's very clever," Pip agreed. "Seb was telling us all about it at breakfast."

Bertie grinned, eyes twinkling. "I can imagine. He's very enthusiastic about the project, you know."

Pip glanced over at Seb, who was leaning his head on Laurence's shoulder. Laurence was resting their entwined hands in his lap. He was still talking to Gavin, and Seb seemed content to listen to the conversation.

"Charlie was just telling me that you two went on a ride together this morning," Bertie said. "I trust it was enjoyable."

Pip looked at Charles, who was grinning slyly at him. "Yes," he said to Bertie. "It was very enjoyable, thank you."

"We had a marvelous talk," Charles put in. "Didn't we, darling?"

Bertie raised an eyebrow before turning to look at Charles. "Did you indeed? Gavin, dear, can you do nothing to curb your husband's horrid propensity for nosiness?"

Gavin rolled his eyes. "You think I could cure him where you couldn't?"

Charles threw back his head and laughed.

"Well," Bertie said, chuckling. "Miracles have been known to happen."

"When it comes to Charles, miracles usually happen because he's done something to move them along," Gavin replied.

Everyone laughed at this. Then lunch was called and they all adjourned to the dining room. They took their lunch leisurely, bantering back and forth about Gerry's wedding, Laurence's garden project, and Charles's nosy disposition.

Eventually the conversation tapered down a bit and Seb asked, "What did you say your project was, Pip?"

Everyone turned to look at Pip and he felt himself flush at the sudden attention. He glanced at Bertie, worried that the other man might be disappointed to know the project was spoken of. Although, as usual, Bertie looked completely at peace with the situation. He gave Pip a small smile and an almost imperceptible nod of encouragement.

"Well, it's to do with Sandellini. Bertie has a quizzing glass of his and we're trying to determine what it does."

"Not that quizzing glass you dragged all over Europe?" Charles said. "That thing has given you no end of trouble."

"Oh, Charlie, no need to exaggerate," Bertie said in a dismissive tone. "There have been a few burglary attempts. But no harm done really."

"You have an original Sandellini?" Laurence said, leaning forward.

Bertie nodded. "Bought it in Florence for a song. Very lucky. But I've never gotten around to solving it, as it were. Pip and I have made a project of it."

Laurence looked impressed. "That sounds fascinating. I hope you'll tell us what you find out."

"To be sure, darling. Although," he added, looking at Pip. "It has been giving us a frightful amount of stick, hasn't it? More than I expected, that's certain. We still haven't the foggiest notion what the silly thing does."

"What do you mean?" Seb said. "Is it meant to do something, other than, well, whatever it is quizzing glasses generally do?"

"Sandellini was adamant about magic having a personality," Laurence said. "His discovery of Constitutional Properties was somewhat revolutionary in its time. But then he went on to expound on the theory in rather extravagant ways." He glanced at Seb's confused face and smiled. "For instance, one of his final experiments was attempting to manipulate a clock so it could magically alter time. That sort of thing. And I believe his final experiment was fatal, although I can't remember what it was."

Bertie waved a hand in an airy gesture. "Something explosive, I remember that much. It was all rather hushed up, you know. Trying to keep other spellcasters from getting ideas."

"So you think this quizzing glass has been magically enhanced in some way?" Gavin said.

"Considering the original owner, yes. I have long been convinced of this fact. However, Pip's doubts as to that are beginning to grow on me," he said, flashing Pip a smile. "It is turning out to be the most stubborn little thing, isn't it?"

Pip did not like the sound of that—Bertie doubting himself was not a pleasant thing to witness. Although he was still not entirely comfortable with the notion of public affection, Pip sacrificed his comfort in order to offer some to Bertie; he laid a hand over Bertie's and gave it a squeeze.

Bertie gave him a soft, knowing smile, undoubtedly recognizing the momentousness of the gesture. "I daresay we'll turn out to be more stubborn, eh, darling?"

Pip smiled and nodded. "I'm sure of it."

He withdrew his hand and glanced shyly around the table. Charles was flagrantly smiling fondly at him, Gavin was studiously staring into his teacup, Seb was blushing and fiddling with his serviette, and Laurence was smiling at them both, although less showily than Charles was. He caught Pip's eye and gave a little wink and then promptly leaned across to Seb and kissed him on the cheek.

"Well, my love, I think we'd better leave them to it."

Seb nodded and tossed the serviette aside. "Absolutely. Besides, now that Bertie has looked the garden over, I'm sure you'll want to act on all of his suggestions."

"Thank you for lunch," Laurence said as he stood. "Good luck with your project," he said to Pip and Bertie. "And do please keep us informed."

"Gladly, darling," Bertie said.

"Good luck," Pip said in reply.

Laurence gave him a warm smile and allowed Seb to lead him away.

"Well," Bertie said. "This has been delightful. Would you like to get back to it, m'dear?"

Pip nodded. They bid their goodbyes to the Kentworthys and headed for the door.

"Oh," Pip said as they passed the library. "Do you mind if I get something before we go?"

"Not at all," Bertie said, following him into the room.

"I asked Seb if we had anything on Sandellini. I thought I might bring them with me and look over them if you do more spells above my ability."

Bertie tsked. "Let's say above your training, dearest; they are certainly within your ability. But what is it you're looking for?"

"I'm not sure," Pip admitted. He pulled the little stack off his bookshelf. "But you know so much about the man and it's that knowledge that makes you so certain about the quizzing glass. I thought if I read up a bit more, I might find some sort of clue."

"Not a bad notion," Bertie said. He glanced at the half empty shelf. "This is a rather hodgepodge collection of books. Should I be teasing Gavin for his library organization?"

"Oh, no," Pip said quickly. "It's my shelf. That's why it's all hodgepodge."

Bertie turned to look at him inquiringly.

"I'm a much better reader than I was when I first came here, of course. But Gerry and Gavin have always been kind enough to put books on this shelf that they think I might like. It...er...it's been nice to have a less daunting selection to go through."

"I can imagine," Bertie said softly. "Trust the Hartfords to think of something sweet like that."

Pip nodded. "Gerry's idea. And Gavin never puts books there in my presence. But I'm pretty sure he does it when no one's looking."

Bertie glanced over the books. "Judging by this edition of Donne's sonnets, I'm inclined to agree with you. You like poetry, my sweet?"

"I do. I don't pretend to fully understand it, but I like its... sound and feel. If that makes sense? I find I can appreciate it more than, say, philosophy books."

Bertie smiled at him. "It does make sense. I confess I've never had the right sensitivity for poetry. I try to avoid admitting as much to Gavin."

"Probably just as well," Pip said, laughing. "But he seems to have forgiven Laurence for that."

"True. Although I rather think that is because Laury is so

dashed easy to get along with. It's hard to hold a grudge against the dear man for anything."

"You're much the same."

Bertie smiled and stroked Pip's cheek with his thumb.

"Ah, you're still here," Charles's voice broke into the quiet moment with such suddenness that Pip jumped and Bertie's hand snapped away from Pip's cheek as if it had been burned. They both turned to find Charles standing in the doorway and grinning hugely. "My word, darlings, no need to stop on my account."

"Charlie, my sweet, you have the most appalling timing. I do hope you have a good reason for it."

"Well, I did want to have a word with you, Bertie," Charles said with mock solemnity. He crossed his arms and attempted to look serious. "You know this young man is under my care, don't you? I trust you'll send him home at a reasonable hour tonight?"

"Don't be absurd. He's of age and you know perfectly well nothing happened."

"I'm not entirely sure what Pip's age is, my dear," Charles countered. "So, as a matter of fact—"

"Next, I suppose you'll be insisting on a chaperone."

"Now that you mention it—" Charles said eagerly.

Bertie rolled his eyes. "Absolutely not. Allow me, darling," he added kindly to Pip as he plucked the books out of Pip's arms and began leading the way out of the room. "Charlie, as my dearest and oldest friend, you know me better than anyone else in the world, so I know you will take this in the best possible light: kindly remove yourself from my business."

"I'm sure I don't know what you mean, dear," Charles said, walking backward to keep pace with Bertie. "What business might that be?"

Gavin walked into the room and took an assessing look

around. "God's teeth, Charles. You aren't teasing them again? You know Gerry threatened to send you a curse if you kept it up. I wouldn't put it past her to actually do it."

"We may not need Gerry to do it, m'dear," Bertie said. "Now, if you'll excuse us?"

Pip hurried out of the room after Bertie amidst Charles's laughter and Gavin's gentle scolds.

"The cheek of the man," Bertie said once they were situated in the carriage. "I am sorry, darling. He is the most dreadful snoop."

"I don't mind," Pip said, laughing. "After seeing how he was with Seb and Gerry, I can't pretend I didn't see it coming."

"I confess I've never been on the receiving end of his humor. So I suppose, in a way, I probably deserve it. I've certainly encouraged him enough in the past."

"I'm sure it would have embarrassed me two years ago. But I rather like knowing he sees me as family, even if it is through teasing."

Bertie smiled and wrapped his arm around Pip's shoulders. "You sweet thing. Of course you're family."

Pip leaned against Bertie's shoulder. "It's my first time having one, you know. And considering how often I go to Charles for advice, I'm sure I can stand him teasing me every now and again."

"It'll get worse, you know. The teasing."

"I know. I imagine he's just trying to push me along, in his way."

Bertie huffed. "Well, he has no call to do that. You have no need to be pushed, darling. I'll have a talk with him, if you'd like."

Pip smiled and sat up and kissed Bertie's cheek. It was becoming easier every time he did it. "Thank you, Bertie. I really don't mind it. I rather think I do need to be pushed and Charles knows it."

Bertie trailed his fingertip down the side of Pip's face. "There is no rush, Pip. On anything. I will never push you to do anything you're not entirely comfortable with. You do know that?"

Pip nodded. "Seb said something the other day. How did he put it? He said that Laurence told him he wanted to spend the rest of his life with him but that he didn't care when the rest of his life began. Seb said he wanted the rest of his life to begin right now." He let out a long breath and looked away from Bertie's gaze. "I find myself in a similar predicament. Only I'm torn between wanting the rest of my life to begin and rather frightened by the prospect of change."

Bertie gently turned Pip's face to look into his. "It is perfectly understandable that you should be frightened after everything you've been through. The rest of your life doesn't have to begin with any particular stage or ceremony. If you wanted to take that trip across Europe with me, I could have us ready to leave within a fortnight."

Pip smiled and caught the hand still on his cheek. "That would not be fair to you. I would never treat you so shabbily."

"Now, darling, I—"

"You deserve better than that. It's not at all fair to ask you to wait for me to be ready, I know, but—" Bertie looked about to interrupt, so Pip kept going. "But I know perfectly well you will without me asking it of you."

The carriage pulled up at the house and Bertie gave a little sigh. He scooped up the books and climbed out of the carriage before offering his hand up to help Pip step down. Pip took his hand, feeling a little fluttery at the gallantry. Bertie kept their hands linked as he led the way into his house and all the way to the study.

"You know," Bertie said as he set the books on the table, "perhaps we might do well to turn to the books for tonight and see what we can turn up."

Pip nodded his agreement. "Though I should warn you, I'm not a very quick reader."

Bertie gave his hand a squeeze in reply. "Let's see what my library has to offer on the subject, shall we?" Still holding onto Pip's hand, he led the way out of the study, stopping first to collect a feather, a bit of chalk, and a wooden slate.

Once they reached the library, Bertie set the slate on the ground with the feather on top and chalked a circle around both. Then he chalked out a sigil and murmured an incantation while doing a complex hand gesture over the spell. Pip felt it take, the unmistakable sensation of magic slotting into place like a key clicking open a lock, the initial whoosh of fire catching on a matchstick, the rightness of a clock chiming the hour.

Bertie then picked up the feather, murmured another incantation and gave it a little flick. The slate lifted off the ground. Bertie held the feather chest high and the slate followed, keeping in line with the feather tip. He slid his free hand back into Pip's.

"That will help us with the heavy lifting," he said as he led the way into the library.

Bertie's library was huge. Pip knew it to be a bit of a local marvel. It was two storeys high with spiral staircases leading to the second level. Bookcases lined the walls from floor to ceiling and tall windows flooded the room with light. Bertie made his way confidently into the room, walking past shelves without a backward glance.

Upon reaching the section he was apparently looking for, he passed Pip the feather with a, "Do you mind, darling?" Pip took it, holding the feather shaft between his thumb and forefinger.

The slate obligingly wafted over by him. Bertie began pulling books off the shelves and stacking them onto the slate. The slate bobbed a little with each addition, but never sank below the feather. It also never tipped one way or the other, as if it was resting on a large, floating table.

When he had pulled a good dozen off the shelves, Bertie declared himself satisfied and took the feather back. He flicked the feather again and the slate glided in front of him. With the feather directing the stack of books, Bertie strolled out of the library with Pip in tow.

Pip helped Bertie to unload the slate. "Would you like me to go clean it up?"

"Oh, goodness me, no, m'dear. It's quite all right. It will last us for a little while longer, I fancy." Thus saying, Bertie set the feather down on the edge of his desk, causing the slate to bob at desk height and stay there. He nodded, satisfied, then turned to the stack of books. "I rather think this would be good for you to start with," he said, handing over one of the books Pip had brought. "This is a full list of Constitutional Properties. If you would be so kind as to look up glass, gold, brass, and metal, I think that will be a good starting point." Bertie passed over a piece of paper, a pen, some ink, and a blotter.

Pip sat down and began his research. Bertie sat opposite and plucked a book off the top of the stack. He seemed to be looking for something particular. He would open the book, flip to a certain section, read for a quarter of an hour or so, then set the book aside and pull off another one. Pip would have felt silly for going so slowly through the one book, except he suspected this was why Bertie had delegated the task to him. He had no idea what Bertie was looking for in the other books. He wanted to be properly thorough, so he wrote down every single detail of each item Bertie had mentioned. His writing was still not the best, so it was slow going. After about two hours, he was done, and he handed Bertie the list.

"Would you like me to take these back to the library?" he said, looking at the pile of discarded books.

"Oh, we can put them on the slate."

Pip stacked them back up on the slate while Bertie read over the list.

"We can put them back in the library and then go and have some tea," Bertie said as he picked up the feather and flicked the stack to float ahead of him. He set the feather on the floor of the library and the slate obligingly settled down as well.

"I'll send someone to put them away later," he said as they walked back to the sitting room.

"Did you find anything?"

"No, unfortunately not."

"I'm sorry. I'm afraid I got us off track a bit."

"Oh, good heavens, m'dear, not a bit of it. You were quite right to take a step back and look at the history of the man. I rather think your side of things will be most helpful, actually. The list of materials, I mean."

"Oh?"

"I'm wondering if I'm going about it all backward. I might try to use the quizzing glass as a component of a spell, as opposed to the focus. I'd like to see if that does anything substantial."

"But mightn't that harm the glass itself?"

"We'll find gentle sorts of spells to cast, not to worry."

They reached the sitting room and Bertie rang for tea before they settled on the sofa. Pip found himself leaning against Bertie's shoulder almost automatically and Bertie obligingly draped his arm around Pip's back. Pip thought he felt Bertie lightly kiss the top of his head.

The silence descended comfortably and Pip found his mind

drifting. He knew so little about Bertie really and it was times like these that he wished he had the courage to ask more. It occurred to him that Bertie had reacted favorably to his recent courage, so he took a deep breath and said, "Will you tell me about your family?"

"Gladly," Bertie said. "Although I'm afraid there isn't much to tell. I had a father who died about twenty years ago. Great man. Dashed clever. Very noble. If the stories I've heard tell of him are true, he lived a very exciting life before he went and got married. I have a mother who still lives in the family seat up north."

"What's she like?"

Bertie chuckled. "She's French and very outspoken in her opinions. Very generous. Very kind. Also very clever. Gerry reminds me of her a great deal, actually. So I daresay after your friendship with her, you'll be well prepared for my mother."

Pip gave a little start. "You think she'll want to meet me?"

"She has been wanting to meet you for two years. I've been putting her off on the matter. If she meets you, she'll be worse than Charles. Best not to open that particular door until we're both good and ready. Not that I anticipate any problems," he went on. "I'm entirely confident she will adore you. Although I should tell you that she will not be so reticent in showing you affection. She is quite affectionate by nature."

"I've often suspected you might be too."

The tea trolley was brought in and Pip sat up.

"I come by it naturally," Bertie continued, giving Pip a wink. "But I don't want you to fret about my mother. She is a powerful personality, but she is already predisposed to like you. She's been angling for an invitation to come visit for simply ages. As I said, I've been putting her off."

"I'm sorry," Pip said as he accepted his tea.

"Don't be. I've gone up to visit her, of course. I'm not a

negligent son or anything. But I have no desire to have her come in and take over. She tends to do that, you see."

Pip nodded and sipped his tea. "No siblings?"

"None. Charlie is the same way. It's one of the many reasons we got on so well. We were both frightfully lonely as children."

"Didn't the dukex come to live with you?"

Bertie smiled. "Yes, Julian moved in after my father died. My mother was, as you can well imagine, grief-stricken and rather overwhelmed with the prospect of managing the estate and me. So Julian came and helped with both in their way. They're practically a parent, really. They had a great deal of influence in my upbringing."

"I can imagine," Pip said, thinking fondly of the Dukex of Molbury. He wondered what they would say if he asked for their advice on how to proceed with Bertie. He realized they'd probably insist on a chaperone being present and be full of suggestions about propriety. The mere prospect of a more formal relationship nearly made Pip shrink in his seat.

It also occurred to him that marriage with Bertie would also mean a more solid connection to Julian. That thought pleased Pip exceedingly. He wondered what having Julian as a more formal relation would be like. He was so caught up in these thoughts that he didn't realize at first that Bertie was speaking to him.

"Anything else you wish to know about my family, dearest?"

Pip smiled, rousing himself from his spiral of thought. "I'll listen to anything you have to tell me. You don't talk about yourself often."

Bertie chuckled and sipped his tea. "I daresay those are the most interesting details. I have an assortment of aunts and uncles and cousins and things. No one else I'm particularly close to."

Pip noticed that Bertie had not really commented on not talking about himself much and he sipped his tea thoughtfully.

Bertie tapped him under the chin. "Care to tell me what you're thinking so ponderously?"

"Just realizing that you and I are not as different as I tend to think."

"Oh?"

"We were both lonely as children, with one very close friend, and we're both very private people by nature." Pip smiled shyly. "I'm afraid I always think of us in terms of our differences, but it is nice to see the similarities."

Bertie gave him a soft smile. "Very astute observations, m'dear. I daresay you are correct. And I suspect it's those similarities, not to mention others as yet unmentioned or undiscovered, that cause us to be—if I may be so bold as to say—so well suited for each other."

Pip was so pleased by this statement that he reached up to cup Bertie's face and pull him close to kiss his cheek.

Bertie covered Pip's hand, as he had done the previous day, and said softly, "You know you're turning out to be of a rather affectionate nature, yourself."

Pip grinned. "You make it easy. I'm only doing things I've wanted to do for ages but was too nervous to do." He rubbed Bertie's cheek with his thumb. "The more I make the attempt, the easier it becomes. I'm quite liking it."

"Oh, as am I, I assure you."

"You are the first man I've ever been with who I genuinely care for and desire. It is such a new sensation. A good one," he added. "A freeing one. Sometimes frightening. But, Lord, Bertie, you make everything so easy."

Bertie leaned forward and kissed him softly on the cheek. Pip closed his eyes in response. Bertie pulled back slowly, as if sensing that Pip might need a break from all the affection.

Pip took a steadying sip of tea. "I know you hate when I talk about him, but when I first started with Jack, I was so very young; I didn't know my own heart or mind at all. And besides, I was turning to him more out of a desperate sort of loneliness."

"Something he took full advantage of," Bertie put in.

"Yes. He was good at that. I'm sorry I'm forever comparing. I'm sure that's unpleasant for you. I don't mean to be. He was... well, he was my entire life for so long, it's hard not to compare everything in my new life to what I experienced with him. Including you."

Bertie ran his thumb along the side of Pip's jaw, looking thoughtful. "I suppose there is an unreasonable part of me that wishes you could scrub him from your mind altogether. But that seems unlikely, doesn't it?"

Pip tilted his head in consideration. "I don't know. I suppose it is unlikely right now because I...I think I'm still a little stuck there. I don't know how to explain it."

"I promise to do everything in my power to get you unstuck, darling."

Pip beamed. "If anyone can do that, it's certainly you." He felt as if the moment called for a kiss—a real kiss. But he didn't feel quite ready for that, so he settled for another kiss on Bertie's cheek. Bertie didn't seem to mind. "So," Pip said after a quiet moment had passed. "What are we doing next? More spellcasting?"

Bertie set his teacup down and poured out more tea for both of them. "I think before we proceed with the next set of spells, I would do well to determine what spells might work best. But I'm not sure that is something I can easily divide between the two of us. So I will work on that m'self later."

"Oh," Pip said. "So what will we do until dinner?"

"Well, if you are not opposed to taking a break from our

project, there are some things around the house I'd like your opinion on."

Pip blinked at him, bemused. "There are?"

"Yes, is that all right?"

"Certainly."

He was exceedingly curious. After they finished tea, Bertie stood up, offered his hand, and walked them both out of the house and to the gardens. He found a young gardener's boy tending to the roses and sent him off to fetch the head gardener. An older man, skin brown with sun, came out to greet them.

"Good day, your lordship," he said jovially. "You asked to see me?"

"Yes, Roberts, I was wondering if you could bring those sketches you showed me earlier."

The man bowed and went off to do as he was asked. Bertie led Pip on a leisurely stroll down the garden path. "My head gardener has some ideas for adding to the gardens and the conservatory. I'd like you to help me decide which plants to select."

"You would?"

Bertie squeezed his hand. "You see, my sweet, I want you to feel as at home here as possible. I can't think of a better way to do that than for you to have a hand in how this home looks."

Pip was floored by the statement. He felt a little overwhelmed by it as well. Finally, he said, "Is this the sort of thing Gavin does with Charles's place?"

Bertie grinned, his gaze still fixed on the path ahead. "I fancy that it is."

Pip was equal parts intimidated and honored by this situation. Bertie was treating him like a husband already.

At length, the gardener came back with a stack of papers in his arm. "Here you are, sir. Which ones would you like to go over first?"

"Oh, I leave that entirely up to you, my good man," Bertie said. "I recall you saying you had several ideas."

The man nodded enthusiastically and walked them to the rose garden. "We have space right here, my lord, for a new bush. Now, we have some options." He pulled out a large sheet and pointed to two different rose sketches. "Myself, I'm partial to these two. I think they'll go beautifully with the others. But of course, we can acquire whichever ones you like best."

Bertie turned to Pip. "What do you think, darling? Any preference?"

Pip contemplated the two sketches. He was grateful the man had narrowed the options down. He looked between the sketches and the roses surrounding the empty space. "I rather like this one," he said. "The colors complement the flowers on either side, I think. Don't you agree?" he said, turning to Bertie.

Bertie smiled and nodded. "To be sure. We'll take that one, Roberts."

The gardener beamed, clearly pleased that his opinion had been taken into account. "I was thinking that these would look very fine over here, sirs. There's this nice bit of wall, you see, and there are some lovely plants that would fill that space." He held up a sketch of a lavender-colored flower. "It was only recently brought to the country," he added. "But I know where I can get some cuttings."

"This is beautiful," Pip murmured. "Will it climb up the wall like it does on the sketch?"

"That it will, sir. Should look very impressive."

Pip glanced at Bertie. The viscount was looking at him expectantly. The decision was clearly Pip's alone. He nodded. "I like it very much."

"Very good," the gardener said. "Now, my next suggestions are for the conservatory."

"Lead on, Roberts," Bertie said.

They strode past the wall and Pip looked at it, imagining the lovely purple flower climbing up the white brick expanse. It was thrilling to think of, and even more thrilling to know it would be his decision that finalized its presence. In the conservatory, Pip agreed to three more plants being added, but decided against the final one Roberts proposed, as he didn't care for the look of it. The gardener hustled off.

"That was very kind of you," Pip said.

"It is my deepest pleasure, darling. Are you ready for another decision?"

Pip nodded.

Bertie led him back to the library. Pip was surprised to note that the spell and books had already been cleaned up in their absence.

"I've been thinking about your little shelf in Charlie's library. I'd like to give you one here too. The question is, where to put it? It can be anywhere you'd like. We can have one emptied close to the door, so you don't have to go very far for it. But I did think it might be pleasant to have one over here by the window." He walked them both over to one of the large windows. "This one, for instance. You could find a book you like and sit on the window seat. But then there's also—"

"Oh, Bertie," Pip said, a little tearfully.

Bertie looked at him in dismay. "My goodness. I haven't offended, have I, my sweet? Oh, do forgive me. I didn't mean—"

Pip quickly took the other man's hand in his. "It's wonderful. You're wonderful."

Bertie let out a breath in evident relief. He pulled out his handkerchief. "I don't mean to rush you, you know. That is certainly not my intention. But it is very important to me that you feel at home here. It occurred to me that if you felt more comfortable here now, then the notion of change wouldn't be quite so daunting."

Pip wound his arms behind the gentleman's back, pulling him into an embrace. Bertie's arms tenderly circled Pip.

Pip sniffed into Bertie's shoulder. "I like the idea of the window seat," he said, although he didn't relax his hold. "But I don't know how often I'd be reading alone in here. I'm sure I'd prefer to read next to you or in your study while you're working."

Bertie's arms tightened around him ever so slightly. "That's a lovely notion, dearest. Perhaps, in that case, we'll find a shelf close to the door?"

"I'd like that very much."

Bertie turned his head to kiss Pip's temple. "Excellent. I'll have Carlisle take care of that straight away."

Pip held him a moment longer and then stepped back, wiping his face with his hands.

Bertie reached up to rub his thumb gently under Pip's eye. "What sort of books do you like other than poetry? It may take me some time to know your tastes."

Pip smiled and shrugged. "I hardly know my tastes myself. I think Gerry picked things that were easiest to read. I've been reading everything that's put on my shelf. But I should warn you again, I'm really not a quick reader."

"You say that as if you think I'll judge you for it."

"I judge myself for it. I'm surrounded by so many clever people. I feel horribly dull-witted by comparison."

"Now, darling, you know that isn't the case."

Pip did not fully agree, but he knew arguing was fruitless. He glanced up at Bertie shyly. "Was that everything you wished to show me?"

Bertie smiled and looked a little self-conscious. "Well, it did occur to me that since you've been blessing me with your good company, it might not be a bad thing to let you help approve the menus. Mx. Benson will be giving me the ones for the following week in the morning."

Pip gaped for a moment. Bertie really was preparing for him to settle there. He was both delighted by it and a little surprised. "I'm not sure I have a preference in the menus," he said at last.

"You must have some things you like more than others? Even if you're too polite to say so?"

Pip chuckled. "If you would like me to take a look at them, I will be glad to do so."

"Marvelous," Bertie said, beaming. "I have something else I would like to show you, but it can wait for another day. I don't wish to overwhelm you. Or think that I am rushing you, by any means."

"I'm not feeling rushed," Pip assured him. "I'm surprised by it. But you were completely correct when you said it would make the prospect of change less daunting. I'm already looking forward to seeing the plants brought in. Especially that one on the wall. What was it called?"

"The wisteria? Yes, I'm quite partial to them myself."

Pip nodded, mentally repeating the word to himself. "What was the other thing you wanted me to see?"

Bertie grinned, clearly pleased. He held out his hand.

Pip took it and allowed himself to be led out of the library and down the hall. Bertie walked past his study to the room beside it. The room was at the back of the hall, and Pip realized that he had barely noticed it before because the door was covered in shadow. But when they walked in, it turned out to be a brightly sunny room with windows lining two walls. Pip could see the garden out of one set of windows. There was an assortment of chairs, settees, and spindly tables.

"This is currently known as the blue salon," Bertie explained. "It's a sort of overflow sitting room, you see. Well, I thought it might suit for a study. We could have a desk put here, and shelves, if you'd like them, or paintings, or whatnot. And whatever seating arrangement you'd like." Bertie turned to him, looking, to Pip's surprise, a little nervous.

Pip was still trying to grasp what Bertie was showing him. "You want this as an additional study?" he said, trying to clarify.

Bertie blushed. "Well, I've always thought it quite a nice arrangement for Gavin to have his own space—where he might have room for whatever papers and documents he goes through. Of course, considering Gavin, we all know he probably spends most of his time reading. But I think every person ought to have a space to call their own. That is, for their own purposes.

"And, of course," he went on hurriedly. "It doesn't have to be this room. But I thought you may not wish to be far removed from my own room. Particularly...particularly at the beginning, you see. And, as I said, there is no rush whatsoever. For I would like you to pick your own paint colors and wallpapers and paintings and such. So it will likely take some time for the room to be ready for you."

Pip looked around the bright little room in wonder. He felt too overwhelmed by the gesture to say anything, but Bertie was looking so apprehensive that he knew he had to say something. He gave Bertie's hand a squeeze and cast about for an appropriate response. "The room is so nice and airy," he said at last. "I feel that a light color would suit it best. Don't you think?"

Bertie's smile was so magnificently beautiful, Pip almost pulled him for a kiss right then and there. "I think that's a marvelous idea. I'll have some paint samples sent over for us to look at."

"Thank you."

"I know a very fine muralist. Perhaps we might have a mural painted on one wall for you. I fancy that would look very nice."

Pip didn't answer, but he wrapped his free arm behind Bertie's back and nestled his head against Bertie's chest as he continued to look around the room.

Bertie seemed to take this as an adequate response. He rested his arm around Pip's waist and let out a long breath, and Pip thought it might be one of relief.

Later, when they sat together for dinner, Pip reflected that he was glad he had talked to Charles that morning. It was strange to have spoken of proposing and the subsequent marriage state and then to see Bertie preparing for that eventuality. He sometimes felt as though Bertie could read his mind—from the way Bertie never pushed him to do anything beyond his comfort to the way Bertie now seemed to sense that Pip was nearly ready. He looked fondly over at the viscount, trying to mentally compose what he might say when he finally was ready to say the necessary words.

Bertie glanced up at him and smiled. "What are you thinking about?"

Pip hesitated a moment before speaking. "I was thinking about you. But I'm not sure I'm ready to put it all into words yet."

Bertie nodded and did not press the issue further.

After dinner, they enjoyed some port and Pip very pointedly did not fall asleep on Bertie's shoulder. "I don't wish to give Charles any more ammunition," he said when he announced that he should leave.

"As if he needs it," Bertie said, walking him to the door.

Pip allowed the footman to help him into his coat. He turned back to Bertie, unsure of how to adequately express what the day had meant to him. Finally, he said, "Thank you for everything."

Bertie smiled knowingly and kissed him gently on the cheek. "A pleasure as always, dearest."

He got home and found Charles and Gavin in the sitting room where they usually read together. Although this time, Pip walked in to see Gavin on his back on the sofa, with Charles practically kissing him into the cushions. The book of poetry was on the floor. Pip very deeply did not want to interrupt them, but he always reported when he had returned home, especially since they always waited up for him. He realized the alternative was to make a servant do it, and that hardly seemed fair. He cleared his throat.

Gavin jumped and blushed a bright red.

Charles, on the other hand, looked wholly unembarrassed. He grinned up at Pip. "Home early tonight, I see."

"Yes, well, I didn't want you to fret, particularly after that lecture you gave Bertie this afternoon."

Charles chuckled and slid his arm so he could rest on his elbow, which allowed him to simultaneously hide Gavin a little from view and leverage himself up a bit to see Pip better. "I certainly appreciate it, darling. I trust you had a nice time?"

"A lovely time. I'll tell you all about it tomorrow."

"Marvelous. Good night, my dear."

"Good night." Pip closed the door behind him and left them to it. He knew that hinting he had something to tell would usually have Charles's mind whirring with curiosity. It was something of a relief to know that the gentleman was happily occupied and his nosiness would not have free rein until much later.

DAY FIVE

The next morning, Pip woke a little early and was the second one in the breakfast room. Charles was already there, eating breakfast and reading a paper.

He smiled up at Pip and promptly put his paper to the side. "I gathered from our brief conversation last night that you had news to impart."

"In a manner of speaking," Pip said as he served himself some food. "But not the news you're thinking."

Charles didn't say anything as Pip sat down, although curiosity was written plainly all over his expression.

Pip chuckled at the sight of it. "Bertie let me pick out some flowers for the garden and the conservatory. And we discussed where he might clear a shelf for me in the library—he was quite taken with the one I have here, you see."

"I see," Charles said, leaning forward. "Do go on, darling."

Pip smiled. "He said he'd like me to approve the menu when I come over today. And…" he hesitated for a moment. "He showed me a room he'd like to have done over to suit my tastes. That is, he'd like to make it another study."

Charles grinned broadly. "My word, you did have a lovely

time." He poured tea for Pip since Gavin was not yet down to do it. "Anything else of note?"

"No, I don't think so," Pip said. And because Gavin was not yet in the room, he added, "But I must say I'm pleased to know that you two really won't be lonely or suffering from lack of entertainment when Seb and I have moved out."

Charles snorted into his teacup.

Gavin walked in at that juncture. "Good God, Charles. I'm not sure I've ever heard you make that sound." He blushed when he looked at Pip. "Good morning, Pip. How are you today?"

"Very well, Gavin. Thank you. How are you?"

"Quite well," Gavin said. He started toward the food and then paused. He turned back toward Pip and wrapped both hands tightly around the back of a chair. Not meeting Pip's gaze, he said, "I fear I should apologize for last night. I'm sure you were not expecting to come home to that."

"I didn't mind."

"That's only because you're being polite. It was—"

"It was highly refreshing to see such things occurring to the mutual pleasure of both parties," Pip said.

Gavin looked up in surprise.

Pip gave him a small smile. "Truly, Gavin. I was not uncomfortable. I hated to interrupt is all. But I didn't wish to send a servant in to do it."

"Not to mention the fact that I deserved to be interrupted," Charles put in.

Pip grinned. "Well, yes. And that."

Gavin's mouth twitched. "Very well. If you're sure you're not bothered—"

"Quite sure."

Gavin nodded and then got his breakfast. As soon as he sat

down, Charles reached for Gavin's hand and tugged him forward to kiss him.

Gavin let him and then said, "Really, Charles. Just because Pip said he didn't mind does not mean we need to carry on in front of him."

Charles smirked but didn't reply. They ate their breakfast in silence until Pip said, "Where's Seb?"

"He went riding with me and then went to have breakfast with Laury," Charles said.

"Goodness," Pip said. "He's wasting no time, is he?"

Gavin gave a snort of his own.

Some time later, Charles left the table, as he had an early appointment in town. As soon as he was gone, Gavin turned to Pip. "You're truly not bothered?"

Pip smiled and pushed his teacup forward on the table. "Truly. Although I don't like to see you embarrassed."

Gavin gave a little huff and then refilled Pip's cup. "I don't like affection in public, but we're not in public. I don't mind it among family."

Pip beamed at him.

"Seb had already gone upstairs. He's exhausting himself working outside every day, you know." Gavin smiled a little, looking fond. "But I wouldn't have allowed it to go so far as... well, as far as it did if I'd known you'd be home so soon. I don't wish to make things unpleasant for you."

"You mean because of my past?"

Gavin nodded, solemn.

Pip sipped his tea. "I suppose if I had seen such goings on when I first arrived, it may have been a shock. But even then I could have appreciated the difference between two married gentlemen and what I've experienced."

Gavin blushed.

"Your respect for each other is evident," Pip said. "It is

nothing like what I used to deal with. If anything, seeing you two makes me yearn for something similar."

Gavin's mouth twitched. "Really?"

"Really. It's just a matter of having the courage to go after it."

"Well, you're one of the most courageous people I know. I have no doubt you'll have it when you're ready."

"Thank you." Pip considered. "Were you...nervous about marriage?"

Gavin leaned back in his seat. "Very. At first it was because I was determined to believe I was unlovable. And I was too afraid to pursue marriage for fear of discovering my beliefs were correct." He took a sip of tea. "After Charles proposed, that fear reduced. Although it has never really gone away entirely."

"I suspect Charles intends to make a project of that."

Gavin's mouth quirked. "Undoubtedly. But in answer to your question, I was still nervous about marriage after he proposed, only for entirely different reasons."

"What reasons?"

"I was nervous about running a household. I was nervous about meeting his family and friends and have them find me wanting or undeserving. I was nervous about my ability to keep him happy...to be honest, I still worry about that. And I was frightfully nervous about the whole aspect of...er...intimacy. I'd never...you understand."

Pip nodded, thoughtful. His mind had snagged on Gavin's mention of running a household. He had only recently become accustomed to living in a grand house such as theirs; he could scarcely imagine what it took to manage one. "How is running the household? Is it as bad as you feared?"

"No, not really. Most of it is talking to the household staff and coordinating things like menus and linen schedules and that sort of thing. I have to play host, you know, serve tea and whatnot. It was a lot to learn. Fortunately, we stayed with my parents for a little while shortly after we became engaged. My mother sat me down and explained a great deal of it. I was still nervous, of course. But I've found that most of it is somewhat mundane and repetitive. I rather like that. And I like knowing the staff well. I find that I get on with them very nicely and that makes everything much easier."

Pip took a sip of tea, pondering all of this.

"And if you're concerned about your own prospects..." Gavin continued, sounding a little hesitant. "Rest assured that I will be glad to teach you everything I know."

Pip looked at him in surprise. "Oh, thank you."

"Although I wouldn't be too worried if I were you. I expect you'll get on famously."

"Charles said something similar. What on earth gives you that impression?"

Gavin gave a small smile. "You are respectful...of everyone. I know that all of our household staff here think very highly of you because of it. Having a genuine respect for your staff is, I find, one of the most important aspects to running a household. After that, I suppose, is some level of organization. After living with you for some time now, I don't foresee any issues there. You're a remarkably tidy person. As for the rest...well, there is a lot to learn, but Charles and I would never send you off unprepared. And Bertie will do everything in his power to make that transition as easy as possible. And besides which, you're very intelligent."

Pip blinked at this little speech. "Thank you," he said again.

"I don't mean to be presumptuous," Gavin said.

"Not presumptuous at all. I did bring the matter up. Besides, I would be very much surprised if you didn't know of my relationship with Bertie by now."

Gavin chuckled. "Then in that case, I think you suit each other admirably."

Pip smiled. "Thank you. I think so too. The primary matter at hand is saying the right words to him."

"That part is always frightening," Gavin agreed. "Although I met a fellow once in London. Actually, Charles introduced him to me. I talked to him when Charles left town. I knew when Charles came back I would need to tell him, as you put it, the right words. At any rate, this fellow told me that everyone is terrified of saying those words, but it's the bold ones that say them anyway." He shrugged. "Of course, Charles came back and I was still terrified, but he sort of encouraged me to say the words anyway. So I did. I was still nervous, but it was worth it."

Pip considered this. One of the many things he liked about Gavin was that the man was of a similar temperament to himself. It was comforting to hear someone else agree that such confessions were, indeed, terrifying. He finished his tea and got up. "Thank you again. You've always had a good knack for getting my head sorted out."

"It's easier to put together a puzzle you've put together before," Gavin remarked.

Pip chuckled and left, making the familiar trek to Bertie's.

He found the gentleman in his study. There was a pile of books on one side of the desk and Bertie was bent over a paper, writing notes and referencing an open book. Since he had missed the opportunity two days in a row, Pip pushed all of his hesitations aside to hop onto the edge of the desk

Bertie smiled up at him. "Good morning, darling! How are we today?"

"Very well. And you?"

"Quite well, quite well. Preparing for our project. I had breakfast," he added with a slight incline of his head.

"Good. I'm glad to hear it. I had a nice chat with Gavin today."

"Did you? Anything of note?"

"Mostly he gave me advice. He's very good at that."

Bertie was looking at him studiously, so Pip did something he'd been too tentative to try before. He lifted his hand and ran it gently through Bertie's hair. Bertie closed his eyes and leaned into the touch.

"Your hair is so lovely," Pip murmured.

"How kind of you to say, my sweet. I confess I've always found it a tad unexceptional."

Pip frowned and shook his head. "It's lovely. All of you is lovely, really."

Bertie opened his eyes, the studious expression still present.

"You're looking very pensive," Pip remarked.

Bertie smiled. "Just thinking."

Pip chuckled and dropped his hand to his lap. He suspected Bertie did not want to speak his thoughts. As Pip could certainly relate to that, he decided not to press. "I feel as though I arrived earlier than you expected."

"Let's say rather I'm a bit behind," Bertie said. "I had several things I wanted to attend to this morning, which meant I started on our project later than usual. But I did send to London for some paint samples. So that was a good thing. And Mx. Benson sent up the menus to be approved." He shuffled through some of the papers on his desk and pulled out a list, which he passed to Pip. "This is everything they intend to cook for the week, you see? Is there anything you don't particularly care for?"

Pip frowned at the paper. "I'm not sure what all of it is," he confessed.

Bertie took the paper back and looked over it. "Hm. I confess that did not occur to me. Well, perhaps I shall tell you what we are eating each night and you can tell me if there is anything you're particularly fond of. How does that sound?"

"I think that will do very nicely."

"Good," Bertie said. He looked over the paper and jotted a note on it. "I'll see to it they get this then."

Pip looked down at the notes Bertie had been writing when he walked in. "I don't think I've ever seen a spell written like this before."

"Calculations," Bertie explained. "I'll have to account for the additional materials that comprise the quizzing glass to ensure they don't alter the spell too much. So I'll be adding other ingredients to counterbalance all of that."

"That's very complicated."

Bertie smiled and gently rested his forearm across Pip's legs close to his knees. He leaned forward slightly and turned his attention to the page of notes. "It is, but I confess I enjoy when magic gets this complex. It becomes a sort of puzzle and I do so love working it out."

Pip grinned at the top of Bertie's head. He ran a hand through Bertie's hair again.

Bertie peered up at him, clearly pleased. "I've been worried that we're going too quickly for you, but I must tell you how much I adore it when you come over all affectionate."

"Don't worry. I've been pacing myself. There are some things I haven't quite worked up the nerve to do, even though I'd like to. And I might add that every time I try something, I enjoy it so much that it gets easier."

"I'm so glad to hear that, dearest."

Pip considered for a moment. "Now that I think of it, I'm not sure I was ever affectionate with anyone else before. Not even with Jack."

"I can't say I'm surprised by that."

"You aren't?"

Bertie shook his head. "You weren't exactly a willing participant with anyone else before. I'm sure you were at the beginning, but you were frightfully young."

Pip brushed hair back at Bertie's temples. "Definitely a willing participant now."

Bertie beamed.

"And it is oddly satisfying to be able to express how I feel even when words fail me."

Bertie's expression turned contemplative and intense at that. He reached up and stroked Pip's cheek.

Pip felt rather arrested by the other man's gaze. He was sure now would be a perfect time to say the words he meant to say, or to put his previous statement to action and give Bertie a kiss. But he couldn't muster up the courage. And though he knew it was cowardly, he decided to deflect. "How did we get on the topic of me again?" he said after a moment. "I thought we were talking about you and your love of complex magic."

Bertie chuckled. He dropped his hand from Pip's face to rest on one of Pip's knees. "That is likely my fault. I have a dreadful tendency to change the subject when I'm the focus. It's an old habit. A bad one, I'm afraid."

"I've noticed. Although you haven't done that as much with me."

"Yes, well, you're different."

Pip was inordinately pleased by this statement. "That's a lovely thing to say. I should add that it doesn't bother me. I mean, I want to know as much about you as possible. But I also understand what it is to be private by nature."

Bertie gave him a soft smile. "I know. It is quite restful, to be honest. You're very undemanding. It makes me more keen to answer questions when you do ask them."

Pip laughed. "How funny. Restful is exactly how I've often described your company."

"I do my best, dearest."

Pip leaned forward and tilted his head to kiss Bertie softly on the cheek. He felt a bit cowardly for it, but consoled himself that kissing Bertie's cheek had felt impossible mere days ago.

Judging by the expression in his eyes, Bertie did not seem to mind.

Pip pulled back and ran his hand through Bertie's hair once more—he was really beginning to enjoy the gesture. "I suppose I ought to stop keeping you from our project," he said.

"Do you hear me complaining, m'dear? I would be more than happy to spend the day doing nothing but this, if you preferred."

Pip considered it. But he glanced over at the calculations and it occurred to him that Bertie had been working diligently to be prepared in time for him and, moreover, had been waiting to solve the mystery of the quizzing glass for years until he was ready. "Perhaps later. When we've worked it out. As you keep reminding me, we have plenty of time for such things. Don't we?"

Bertie smiled brightly up at him. "Indeed we do, darling." He turned to look down at his notes. "However, I still have some work left to do before I'm ready to begin the first spell. To be honest, I'm not sure I'll be done before lunch."

"No hurry on that, as far as I'm concerned," Pip said. "Is there anything I can do to help?"

Bertie shook his head. "Sadly no. I'd explain to you what I'm doing if you'd like, but I suspect you have only a middling interest in this sort of thing."

"You're not wrong. I still remember how horrified I was when Gerry first introduced calculations to my magic lessons."

Bertie chuckled. "I recall. But I don't wish to be remiss in my duties as host either. Perhaps—oh!"

Pip raised his eyebrows in surprise.

Bertie smiled. "Here, come with me." He stood up and held out his hand to help Pip down from the desk.

It was not an overly large desk, but Pip accepted the offer and held onto Bertie's hand as he was led out of the study and into the library.

"I had Carlisle work on it first thing this morning," Bertie said as they walked into the large room. "And I gave him a small list of titles to add to it."

It was the first shelf in the room. Pip noticed that the shelves above and below had been reorganized as well, to include busts and paintings and knickknacks. It made his own mostly empty shelf less noticeable. He grinned as he swept a hand across the wood.

"I love it, Bertie."

He looked at the books Bertie had selected for him. He pulled out one that intrigued him—a slim volume about Paris. He flipped it open to see illustrations of a city he'd only ever heard of. "What is this?"

"It's a travel book. I can't say I recommend most of them as they tend toward overly sentimental language. But that author is rather good. I thought you might look through it and mark anything of interest. That way when we do go, we'll have some idea of what you'd like to see."

"Bertie, I..." Pip felt at a loss for words.

"I have others by the same author," Bertie continued. "She doesn't cover all the cities I'd like to take you to, sadly, but there are a few. At any rate, it should be enough to be going on with."

Pip traced fingertips across the cover of the book. "This makes the notion of travel seem so much more real."

"Well, I confess that was part of my intention as well. I want to impress upon you that my offer was genuine. And I imagine you haven't had much opportunity to learn about other places as you might have liked, so—"

Pip leaned up and kissed Bertie's cheek. "Thank you."

"My goodness, my sweet. It really was nothing."

"Not nothing."

"Would you like to read that while I work?"

"Yes, please."

Bertie nodded and took his hand and walked them back to the study. He brought pillows over to the settee so Pip could lie back and read at his leisure.

Pip was pleased to note that Bertie had placed everything so they were still facing each other. He settled in and started reading, enjoying the fact that he could look up from time to time and watch Bertie working. He was struck by how perfect it felt, and yet how perfectly ordinary it was at the same time. He wondered if this was what it might be like to live with Bertie. He found himself distracted by that line of thought. He leaned against the back of the settee and sorted through his thoughts.

Why was he still so terrified to ask Bertie to marry him? As he had already explained to Charles, he knew he had nothing to fear from Bertie in terms of intimacy. He was fairly sure he wasn't quite ready for that yet, but he was also confident Bertie would not expect it of him. He imagined coming home from work to find Bertie at his desk and going in to dinner together. And evenings spent in the sitting room drinking port and talking, or reading, or simply sitting as they liked to do. He imagined curling up next to Bertie in bed, and found the prospect was comforting rather than terrifying. He thought of the little study Bertie was preparing for his benefit. He was definitely still daunted by the idea of being in charge of running a house and playing host. But then, would putting off the proposal make that any less daunting?

He closed the book and pondered. He had to be honest with himself and admit that he was a little reluctant to move out of Charles and Gavin's house. He loved how familiar it all was. But then, with Gerry gone and Seb on his way out too, it was simply not the same. He didn't like the idea of overstaying his welcome. And he didn't like the idea of rattling about, keeping Charles and Gavin from late-night kisses and fond embraces. Perhaps it was time to move on. He began mustering up the courage to break the silence with bold words.

The butler, Mr. Foster, came in to announce that lunch was ready.

"Excellent timing," Bertie said. "I think I'm done with this part."

Pip gave a small sigh. Perhaps it wasn't time to move on quite yet.

"I'd ask you how you were enjoying the book," Bertie said as they sat down. "But I noticed you were in a bit of a brown study. Imagining travels to foreign climes?"

Pip smiled. "I'm enjoying it. But I was having difficulty focusing."

"Anything you care to discuss?"

Pip did not think over lunch was the sort of moment he had in mind. But he didn't want to evade the question entirely. "I was imagining how often we might find ourselves sitting together in that manner." At sight of Bertie's contemplative expression, Pip hastened to add, "It was a pleasing notion."

Bertie grinned. "I confess I found it so myself."

Pip asked Bertie about the calculations he'd been doing and Bertie accommodatingly explained the spell he intended to use and how he intended to alter it for their purpose. It was a little over Pip's head, but Bertie was patient and careful about explaining things clearly.

After lunch, they returned to the study and Bertie proceeded to set up the spell. It was very complicated. Bertie placed several things together, including the quizzing glass, drew a large circle around them, chalked a sigil inside, and then chalked a bunch of numbers and symbols around the edge of the circle. Then he placed more ingredients around the edge of the circle, chalked another sigil and more symbols and numbers, and chalked another circle around that. Finally, he stepped back.

"There. That ought to do it."

Pip held his breath as Bertie muttered an incantation over the outer circle and moved his other hand over the inner circle and did two separate hand gestures. The plain metal rod inside the inner circle took on a shimmery sheen. Bertie waited for a moment and then sighed.

"It's not what you wanted?" Pip said.

"Well, it did what it was supposed to do. But nothing more than that. It's an illusion spell, you see. They're difficult at the best of times, but adding in all of those other items made it doubly challenging."

"Would it—" Pip broke off.

Bertie looked at him. "Yes, my sweet?"

"Would it be too much trouble for me to ask you to perform it again, but with the usual ingredients? Not the quizzing glass? I'm curious to see the difference."

"No trouble at all." Bertie carefully wiped out all the sigils and the chalk circles and put everything aside.

Pip picked up the quizzing glass while Bertie prepared the spell again. He studied the little accessory. Why was such an ordinary thing causing them so much stick? He stared at the signature on the rim, willing it to tell him something important. It didn't. When Bertie announced that he was ready, Pip nodded to indicate he was paying attention and prepared his senses to feel the spell.

It took significantly less time for Bertie to cast when he only had to worry about the one circle. The metal rod took on the shimmery sheen once again.

Pip twirled the quizzing glass by its handle, irritated that the spell felt exactly the same as it had before. He was impressed, though; Bertie had clearly done a good job with his calculations. Then a flicker of light caught his eye. He frowned down at the quizzing glass and twirled it again. The same flicker of light danced just out of view. Tentatively, he held the quizzing glass up to his eye and gasped.

Bertie looked up at him.

Pip had never seen anything like it. Every item in the circle was shimmering with some sort of pattern or color. The chalk circle and sigil looked bolder and brighter. He stared, trying to figure out what the shimmers and colors reminded him of. Pip pulled the glass away to look at the spell without it. Wordlessly, he handed the glass to Bertie.

Bertie held it up to his eye. "By Jove," he whispered.

"I think," Pip ventured. "I think the quizzing glass allows a person to *see* magic."

Bertie gave a shocked little laugh and then covered his mouth. "How extraordinary." Then he recovered from his shock and abruptly plucked a feather out of a jar on his shelf. He passed the quizzing glass back to Pip.

Pip watched through the glass as Bertie performed a Motion levitation spell, causing a book to float off his desk. Through the glass, Pip saw swirls of light pouring from the feather and lifting the book off the desk. Bertie plucked the book out of the air and placed it back on the desk. He handed the feather to Pip, and Pip passed the glass back over to him and performed the same spell. Bertie laughed at the sight.

"How marvelous!" he said.

Pip brought the book down again and put the feather on top of it. "How on earth did he accomplish such a thing?"

"I have no idea," Bertie said, inspecting the glass. "He really was far ahead of his time."

"He must have been. I don't think anyone else has made anything like it."

"No one else has even come close. And I'm pleased as anything that you worked it out."

"It was more or less an accident."

"Don't dismiss your talents, darling. It was instinct. Why, we should work on these sorts of projects more often. You're brilliant. Do you know? You are positively extraordinary."

Once again, Pip found himself full of emotions and bereft of the proper words to convey them. Without pausing to think it through, Pip framed Bertie's face with both hands, leaned forward, and kissed him.

Bertie was clearly surprised by it and Pip had a moment of panic that he had grossly miscalculated. But then Bertie's arms were encircling him, pulling him closer, and Bertie was kissing him back as sweetly and tenderly as Pip had always known he would. It was unlike any kiss he had ever experienced. It wasn't bruising or possessive or heated, but gentle and reassuring. Pip felt an unexpected urge to cry and pulled back to avoid such an embarrassment. Bertie's arms were still around him and he smiled down at him fondly.

"Was that another instance of affection making up for loss of words?" he asked softly.

Pip nodded.

"Well, I hope you know I agree," he said with a lightly teasing tone.

Pip huffed and ducked his head, a little embarrassed.

Bertie dropped one arm from around Pip's back and gently lifted Pip's chin. "I love you too, petal."

Pip risked the threat of tears and kissed Bertie again. Bertie moved his hand to cup the side of Pip's face and kissed him back.

Eventually, Pip pulled away again and dropped his hands

from Bertie's face in order to wrap his arms around Bertie's waist and lean against his chest. Bertie slid his hand around Pip's back again and they stood silently for a long moment.

Finally Pip said, "I very much appreciate that you don't mind long silences."

He felt Bertie chuckle. "Silence can be very companionable if shared with the right person. Would you like to sit?"

Pip nodded and pulled away. "Perhaps we could have tea?"

"Wonderful notion. Shall we go to the sitting room then?"

Pip slid his hand into Bertie's, noticing then that Bertie still had the quizzing glass chain draped around his other hand. "And we can discuss our discovery."

"Yes, I would like to do that. It does boggle the mind, doesn't it?"

They walked to the sitting room and Bertie rang for tea and sat in the corner of the sofa. He raised his arm so Pip could settle in close to him. Pip adored that and happily accepted the invitation without a word.

Bertie held up the quizzing glass contemplatively. "I wonder if any of the others know what it does," he mused.

"What others?"

"The ones who have tried to steal it."

"Oh. Like the man who hired Jack?"

"Yes, and he wasn't the first. Mind you, I have other magical valuables in my collection, so I suppose they could have been after something else. But I have wondered for years what other people might know."

"Is that why you asked Jack who hired him?"

"Yes," Bertie said. "I had hoped to talk to the fellow and see what I could learn."

"But the other man might have been a powerful spellcaster!"

Bertie scoffed. "Couldn't have been all that powerful or he wouldn't have hired someone to do his dirty work."

The tea arrived and Pip sat up to allow Bertie to pour out. "Bertie?" he asked suddenly.

"Yes, m'dear?"

"Do you think you could show me how to...how to pour tea?"

Bertie turned to look at him with a broad smile. "Gladly. Would you like me to show you now? Or perhaps tomorrow? We did make some life-altering discoveries today."

Pip grinned at him, relieved. "Tomorrow would be perfect."

"I expect we'll want something to do," Bertie said cheerfully. "Now that our project is complete."

"Oh dear," Pip said as he accepted his cup of tea. "It is, isn't it?"

"Well, I shouldn't say that," Bertie said, patting his knee. "After all, I have a great deal of experimenting I'd like to do. So many notes I shall have to take. Perhaps it will be best if Seb were here. He takes very good notes, you know. Better penmanship than mine, really."

"What do you want to do with it?"

"Well, I'd like to compare the looks of different magics. I want to know if it is unique to each spellcaster, each spell, or each ingredient, or all three. After that, I shall have to study the item itself, now that I know what it does. I want to know how he managed it, and if the magic of the quizzing glass is contained in the glass itself or if it has to do with the whole of the structure."

"You want to replicate it?"

"That would be wonderful. It might be impossible, but I'd certainly like to try."

Pip took a sip of tea and considered this. "Didn't you say you were working on another magical tool?"

"Yes. Not nearly as impressive as this, though."

"What will it do?"

"It's actually something of a similar concept. I'm designing a sort of tuning fork that will vibrate in the presence of magic. I'm trying to replicate the feeling of magic that you and I have developed."

"That's wonderful, Bertie!"

Bertie gave a little huff as he sat back against the sofa. "Sadly, it pales in comparison to Sandellini's work."

"Don't say that. I don't think it does at all. Will you tell me about it?"

Bertie smiled. "Well, my idea is to have the thing vibrate when it senses magic. Ideally, a spellcaster could use it to determine if a spell is properly balanced. It might also help spellbuilders to know when a spell has reached an optimal potency. Might cause less waste and help spellcasters from overloading their spells. Granted," he added, "Gerry would have little need for it. I have yet to teach her how to feel magic, but she's always had a good eye for balanced spells."

"But it would be useful to an apprentice who's learning," Pip said. "It would certainly make things a little safer."

"That was my thought, too. There are precious few people who can feel magic, and it is very difficult to train for. It really does make such a difference in spellcasting."

"Do you plan to train more people?"

"I'll train anyone who asks," Bertie replied. "I've talked to Laury about it. I know he's interested, as is Gerry. Although we've discussed that it will have to wait until his work is more along the line of correspondence. It's not the sort of training one can drop and pick up again easily. I think Seb would take to it well, but I'm not sure he's particularly interested, other than out of curiosity."

"What about Gavin and Charles?"

Bertie chuckled. "Charlie will be the first to tell you that he has little talent for magic. Gavin, on the other hand, is a very strong spellcaster. I'm sure he would not consider himself as such, but Gerry used to send him her spells when she was just beginning spell-building and he did a marvelous job with them. Well, there was one unfortunate incident—but that was really more from lack of precautionary measures than from lack of ability. Very impressive family, the Hartfords, really."

Pip considered this. "Do you think their older brother and their parents have the same talent?"

"I think it very likely. And I expect if Gerry has children, there is a strong chance they will grow up to be powerful as well —particularly with Basil as her husband. The Thornes are another magically talented family. The little ones are too young to determine just yet, but I'm looking forward to seeing how many of them grow into their power."

Pip had never thought about magic being a hereditary sort of talent. He'd had little cause to wonder about his birth parents. He'd been left on his own when he was little more than a baby. Very few people in the poorer classes managed to learn magic, as the tools and equipment were costly, and getting an education was often out of reach or of little priority compared to earning enough to eat. Were his parents powerful spellcasters? How many strong and talented people were stuck in the slums of London for lack of resources and education?

He felt a light tap under his chin.

"You're wool-gathering, I think," Bertie said. "Anything you care to share?"

"Just thinking about my own family," Pip said slowly. "It never occurred to me to wonder if my parents had magical abilities."

"Well, everyone has the ability to do magic. Some, like Charlie, can cast spells but can only pour a small amount of power into them. I expect your parents, or at least one of them, must have had a good amount of innate power, whether or not they knew it."

"I imagine many others are the same."

Bertie nodded. "It is a sad reality. I do hate to see good talent going to waste. I know one of Laury's goals is to make magic accessible to more people. I daresay he will manage to do a lot of good if he succeeds."

Pip sipped his tea thoughtfully.

Later, they returned to the study and Bertie did more experimentation, alternating between casting spells and having Pip cast spells so he could watch with the quizzing glass. By the time they sat down to dinner, Bertie was practically giddy with enthusiasm.

"I shall have to make a list of spells to try," he said. "Would it bother you if I invited Laury to come look at it?"

"Why would it bother me?"

"Well, it is our project."

Pip laughed. "It's your quizzing glass. I'm glad to finally know what it does. I've wondered what all the fuss was about ever since...well, ever since we met. And I should like to know what you learn about it and possibly use it from time to time. But I don't have any issue with you showing it to whoever you'd like. Nor will I mind if you continue to experiment when I'm not here," he added. "Because I imagine you'll fret about that as well."

Bertie smiled. "You sweet thing. You do know me well."

After dinner, they sat and enjoyed their port in the sitting room, just as Pip imagined they would do when they were married.

"Perhaps I'll invite everyone over for dinner. I'd like to show Gerry too, but I'm not sure if she'll be interested in coming out for a dinner party immediately after returning home."

"I imagine if you tell her what you'll be showing at the dinner party, she'll come with or without her husband," Pip remarked.

Bertie laughed. "You're probably right. Do you like the idea of a dinner party?"

"Who will you be inviting?"

"Oh, I think I'll keep it to a small gathering. Charlie, Gavin, Gerry, Basil, Seb, Laury, and us."

Pip felt quietly overjoyed by Bertie's casual description of them as a set. But all he said was, "My favorite people. I think that will do quite nicely."

"Very good. I'll send out the invitations tomorrow morning."

When it was finally time to go, Pip stood and reached up to cup Bertie's cheek and pull him down for another kiss. It felt glorious to finally be able to do it. Bertie obligingly wrapped one arm around Pip's waist and reciprocated. Pip left in Bertie's carriage and thought, not for the first time, that it would be nice to stay with Bertie at the end of the day.

He arrived home to find Gavin and Charles reading together on the sofa and very definitely not kissing. They were back to sitting with Gavin using Charles's chest as a personal bolster and Charles reading over Gavin's shoulder.

"You're home much too early these days," Charles remarked when Pip walked in. "I regret saying anything at all."

Gavin raised an eyebrow and turned to look up at Charles.

Pip laughed. "So you should."

DAY SIX

The next morning, Seb joined the Ayles family for breakfast again, so it was just Pip, Charles, and Gavin at the table.

"Do you know," Pip said as he sat down. "I'm rather sad that Seb's been dining out every morning. I feel as though I miss him already."

Gavin nodded. "I always knew you would all move out eventually, but I think there was a small part of me that expected you to live here forever."

"It's a good thing Veronica is no longer here," Charles commented. "She'd put in a very long sermon about how children are helpful in times like these."

Gavin rolled his eyes at the mention of his sister-in-law. "That she would."

"How *is* your brother's family?" Pip asked politely.

"I couldn't tell you," Gavin said. "I try to avoid reading his letters."

"He's doing well," Charles said. "Although Veronica has caught a chill that keeps her in bed most days, which is most unfortunate for her."

"Oh, that's why Father said he's been enjoying the quiet lately," Gavin said. "I did wonder."

Charles chuckled. "I believe little John is doing well. Actually, Gavin's mother provides a more adequate report on his wellbeing than John does. I don't think John knows how to report on his child."

Pip fancied that Charles sounded a little sad as he said this.

"Will they have more children, do you think?" Pip said.

"I don't believe so," Gavin said. "I don't think John particularly cares for children. Well, that is, I'm sure he loves his son, but he doesn't really understand him. And he isn't fond of the noise and mess children tend to create. He has an heir. That's likely all he really worries about."

Pip nodded, feeling as though he might understand Charles's sadness.

"Do you want children, Pip?" Charles asked.

"What?"

"Oh, Charles, really," Gavin said.

Pip considered the question. "I suppose it never occurred to me that I might have the option."

"Oh, you certainly have the option," Charles said, grinning.

"I shall have to mull it over."

"And by 'mull it over,' do you mean talk to Bertie?"

Gavin rolled his eyes.

"I think I'd need to determine what my feelings are on the matter before I bring it up to him," Pip said. "I'm also not sure I'd have the nerve to bring it up."

"His mother will certainly do it if you don't."

"Will she?"

"She's been on to him to get married and have children for years now."

"Oh," Pip said. "What's she like?"

Charles gave him a broad smile. "She will absolutely adore you, darling."

"That is not precisely what I meant."

Charles sipped his tea, still grinning.

"Ignore him," Gavin said. "Seb and Gerry are properly squared away and he has no one else left to push into matrimony."

"Pip was kind enough to remind me that some of the Thorne children are getting close to the right age for such conversations."

Gavin groaned.

Charles laughed and stood up. He leaned over Gavin, lifted his chin, and kissed him softly on the lips. "You know you adore it."

"I wish I didn't."

"No, you don't."

Gavin sighed and then leaned up to kiss Charles again. Charles ran a hand through Gavin's hair and then strode to his study.

"I suppose it's silly to ask if you're going to Bertie's today?" Gavin said after Charles had gone.

"Do you mind?" Pip said.

Gavin gave a small smile. "Of course not. I'd worry that it was from failure on our part to entertain you, but I know better."

"Good. He's planning to invite everyone for dinner tomorrow night."

"Is he?" Gavin hesitated. "Does he have something to announce?"

Pip smiled. "Sort of, but not what you're thinking."

"Your project then?"

Pip nodded.

"You solved it?"

He nodded again.

"So what will you do today?"

"I'm not sure about the whole of it. But I asked Bertie to teach me how to serve tea."

Gavin's mouth quirked. "It's a good thing Charles isn't here. He'd pounce on that little tidbit."

Pip laughed. "Don't I know it." He paused. "Gavin."

Gavin met his gaze, solemn and patient as always.

"I think I might ask him today. And I'm terrified. But I don't even know why I'm terrified anymore."

Gavin looked thoughtful. "It's always frightening to lay your heart bare. And even more frightening when your heart has been poorly treated by others." He leaned forward in his seat. "So, I think your fear is perfectly reasonable. But I also think you know as well as I do that Bertie will not abuse your heart in such a way. If anything, he'll do everything in his power to protect it."

Pip took a deep breath and let it out slowly. "I wish I had more to offer him."

"More than your love, you mean?"

"Yes. I have nothing other than that. I am...nobody. I have no wealth and no title and no parentage. He could have anybody he wanted. If I had *something* to bring to the marriage, other than myself, I'm sure I'd feel better about it."

Gavin nodded his understanding. "I've been fretting for weeks about the inevitability of everyone moving out. I keep worrying that as soon as there are no guests, Charles will realize that all he has left is me." He gave a small self-effacing smile. "I've spent the past few years consoling myself that, at the very least, I was able to give Charles a family like he's always wanted —well, I gave him my family." He shrugged. "Now? My family has all but moved out. I have no idea how much of my dowry is spent or unspent since I don't handle the accounts. Even if I bought him gifts, they would be purchased with his own money. All I have left to offer is my love. Funnily enough, it's the thing I thought might be least valuable and yet it's the only thing that still remains."

Pip could think of no adequate response. Gavin didn't seem to need one. He nodded again with his usual small smile and left the room.

Pip sat in the quiet for a moment and then got up to leave. He passed Charles and Gavin outside the door to the breakfast room. Charles was holding Gavin tightly in his arms and kissing him with evident tenderness. From the letter clasped in Charles's hand, Pip surmised Charles had intended to walk into the room and had overheard some of the conversation. He hurried past them, careful not to interrupt.

He considered Gavin's words the whole walk to Bertie's house. When he reached the house, he realized belatedly that he had been so wrapped up in what Gavin had said, that he had neglected to properly work out what he ought to say. He walked into the house, irritated with himself. He was informed that Bertie was in the library. Pip made his way to the large room.

"Up here, darling!" Bertie called from the second storey.

Pip slowly walked up the winding stairs, realizing, suddenly, that he had never had cause to go to the second storey of the library. "I don't think I've ever been up here before," he said when he reached the top.

Bertie grinned. "That's likely because when I bought the house, I had all of the books I was least interested in moved upstairs."

Pip walked to the banister and looked across the library. "So, why are we up here?"

"I want to see if I have any books on etiquette."

Pip turned to look at him in surprise. "Etiquette? Whatever for?"

"For the tea. I wish to teach you correctly."

"Oh, I'm sorry. I didn't realize it would be—"

"It isn't any trouble. I just wish to ensure I'm pointing you in the right direction. One gets lazy or sloppy over the years. With close friends, it hardly matters, of course. But if one were to ever entertain in more formal situations, then it would do well to know the right way of things."

"Oh," Pip said again. "Are...er...formal situations likely to happen?"

Bertie gave him an apologetic smile. "I'm afraid it's highly possible. Remember all those aunts and uncles and cousins I mentioned the other day?"

"You expect them to visit?"

"Well, if you were asking to learn about tea for the reason I think you were asking, then yes, I expect they will visit."

"Right. So etiquette lessons today, is it?"

Bertie smiled. "Not all day, I'm sure. There's only so much tea one can drink, you know."

"Speak for yourself," Pip said in mock offense. He was, in truth, absolutely horrified by the prospect of well-to-do relations coming to visit and viewing his hosting skills critically. But he didn't want to admit as much to Bertie.

"My goodness," Bertie said. "I was so caught up in my search that I didn't greet you properly." He laid his book on a nearby table and wrapped one arm lightly around Pip's waist. "How are you today, my sweet?"

By way of response, Pip kissed him, feeling his anxieties drifting out of focus. He suspected this was Bertie's intention and he loved the man all the more for it.

Bertie smiled when they broke apart. "That good, eh?"

Pip chuckled. "Did you find what you were looking for?"

"Yes," Bertie said, scooping up a book. "I think this will do. And I think when all is said and done, dearest, I will likely invite my mother here, alone, first. She will not expect formality, but she is an expert at it."

Pip felt anxiety bubbling in his stomach at the thought of being perceived by an expert on formality (other than Julian). Bertie must have noticed, for he took Pip's hand to lead them both downstairs and said, "No matter what happens, you do know you will certainly not be left to weather it alone, right?"

"I know," Pip said. "I'm just worried that your family will think—"

"My family," Bertie said, cutting him off. "Is comprised of my mother, Julian, you, and all of our dearest friends here. I have a great many relations, some of whom are great bothers. I do not intend to invite *them* anywhere. The rest of my relations are quite nice when you get to know them, but can be a little stuffy, at least at first. So a good first impression will go a long way towards making things more pleasant in the long run."

Bertie reached the bottom of the stairs and turned to face Pip while he was still one step up on the staircase. It meant that Pip was, for once, at Bertie's height. Bertie tucked the book under one arm and reached up to cup Pip's face gently.

"Please do not fret about it, m'dear. I promise I won't invite anyone anywhere until you are completely comfortable."

"That's why we're starting tea lessons."

"Exactly."

"Which was my idea," Pip added.

Bertie smiled. "Well, I know you didn't exactly have this in mind when you proposed the lessons. And we certainly don't need to start with everything. But I do wish to teach you the proper way of it, if I'm going to teach you at all."

Pip leaned forward and kissed him, pleased by the fact that he could do so without tilting his head up. He pulled back and grinned. "This is quite a nice little spot, don't you think?"

Bertie laughed. "You darling thing. I daresay I'm wholly in favor of staircase kisses."

Pip kissed him again, briefly, and then stepped down to the ground. He reached up to take the book Bertie had tucked under his arm. "Tea?"

Bertie squeezed his hand. "Tea."

Tea lessons were not as bad as Pip feared. Bertie read through a section of the book before starting. "We'll worry about order of precedence later," he said. "For now, we will focus on the order of the actual tea service."

Pip learned how to pour, how to add sugar and milk. It was tricky handling such delicate things and ensuring the liquid didn't splash onto the saucers. He learned what order all of the food should be served in, how to handle pastries, and how to cut cake.

After about two hours, Bertie declared himself satisfied.

"You already conduct yourself very properly when it comes to holding the teacup and everything," Bertie said. "You've always been a very fast learner when it comes to activities."

"I have?"

Bertie smiled and patted his leg. "Yes, darling. You learned practical spellwork very quickly. And Charles told me how quickly you picked up riding. I daresay, if you wished to learn more athletic activities, you would likely excel."

"Me?" Pip said. "Athletic?"

"You have good command of your body," Bertie said. Then he blushed. "I mean to say, you...well...dash it all, darling, you know what I'm trying to say."

Pip laughed and kissed Bertie's cheek. "I do know. But it is still hard to imagine myself an athlete."

"Oh, I don't know. I think you'd make a fine fencer. And I've long wondered how you'd do with dancing."

Pip felt a small jolt of panic. "Oh, dear."

"What is it?"

"I shall have to learn dancing after all, won't I?"

"Not if you don't wish to…"

"But if there are formal situations?"

"It will certainly help. I imagine we will attend functions with dancing eventually. However," he went on. "I think we have enough friends among us who could keep you properly busy so you wouldn't have to dance with anyone you do not know."

Pip brightened. "Really?"

"Oh, yes," Bertie said. "I adore dancing. So I will gladly dance with you as much as you like. Seb loves to dance, but poor Laury is not a good dancer, so I imagine Seb would be pleased as anything to dance with you. Charlie is, of course, a very good dancer. He would certainly stand up with you. Gerry too. And I know Julia Hearst likes to dance."

"That's all right then," Pip said.

"If we go to any dances outside of Tutting-on-Cress, I shall simply keep a tight hold of you and tell every dashing stranger that I will not permit you to stand up with anyone but me."

Pip laughed. "Do you know you're perfectly wonderful?"

Bertie blushed, pleased.

Pip reached up to cup Bertie's cheek and pulled him in for a kiss. All of their previous kisses had been brief and gentle. This time, Pip did not pull back, but continued to deepen the kiss. He brought his other hand to frame Bertie's face as he did so.

Pip knew himself to be a good kisser. He had, in a way, spent years being trained to kiss well, and then years after being paid for it. Granted, all those other kisses had never been initiated by him and he never desired them. But all the same, Bertie had not been incorrect in his earlier statement that Pip had good command of his body. He knew how to use his lips and tongue to give another man pleasure. And for the first time in his life,

Pip used this knowledge to give the first man he truly loved the benefit of his education.

He felt Bertie gasp a little and then melt and wrap his arm around Pip's waist to pull him closer. Bertie's other hand came to rest tentatively on Pip's shoulder. Pip decided quite suddenly and quite firmly that he wanted that tentative hand in his hair. He wanted Bertie to personally erase all his horrid memories by creating new ones, better ones. He pulled himself closer, deepened the kiss even more. Bertie's hand slid into his hair, almost of its own accord.

Then, Bertie stiffened and pulled away. "Good heavens, my darling. Do forgive me. I'm afraid I completely forgot myself."

"What?" Pip said, bewildered.

Bertie was flushed and looked ashamed. "I'm so sorry, dearest. I told myself I would never—and here I am, forgetting—" He stood and rubbed a hand over his face. "It was completely reprehensible."

"Bertie, you're not making any sense," Pip said. He was at a loss. Had Bertie not liked the kiss?

Bertie seemed to be trying to compose himself. "Your hair, darling. I promised myself I would never touch it, no matter how sweet you look with it curling about your face. I remember quite distinctly how much that wretched man favored it and I vowed long ago not to be anything like him."

Pip stood and touched Bertie's arm. Bertie clasped his hand. "I do hope you can forgive me, Pip. I promise I won't—"

"Bertie, sit down for a moment," Pip said softly.

Bertie looked bewildered, but he did as Pip asked.

Pip took a deep breath. Hadn't Charles mentioned something about kneeling? He knelt slowly in front of the sofa and took both of Bertie's hands in his. "Bertie, you did nothing wrong. I promise. I wanted you to touch my hair. I did some amount of maneuvering to encourage you to do so."

"You did?"

"Yes," Pip said, smiling. "That was, without a doubt, the best kiss I have ever experienced."

Bertie blushed. "Very sweet of you to say so, but I'm afraid you were doing most of the work."

"I know," Pip said with a laugh. "Do you know why? Because, for the first time, I actually wanted it." He paused and sat back on his heels, collecting himself. "You know I have many painful memories. Horrible ones. Ones that still haunt my dreams occasionally. You said the other day that you wished you could scrub all those memories away for me. And I just realized that I want that, too. I want to replace every single horrible memory with five wonderful ones. And I have a great many of them, so we have quite a lot of work to do."

He took a breath. He didn't think he was doing this right at all. "I'm sorry. I was sure I should have planned this beforehand." He didn't meet Bertie's gaze as he pressed on. "I've spent the past few days trying to drum up the courage to say the words...t-to tell you that I want to make you feel as wonderful as you make me feel. I want to spend the rest of my life trying to find out what will make you happiest. I want to see the world with you, but my world has never been more complete since you came into it. I—"

A tear fell onto his cheek. "I want to wake up next to you each morning and spend afternoons reading in your study while you work. I want to make it my personal duty to see that you never work through a meal again. I want to keep learning from you. I want to keep learning about you. I want to fall asleep on your chest and then go upstairs to bed with you. I want to use all this ridiculous knowledge I have to give you as much pleasure as possible and I want—"

Tears were falling more steadily now. He was decidedly not looking at Bertie as he spoke. "I want you to know that even though I have nothing to offer you, I have nothing in my possession and no family or titles or anything—I have nothing, Bertie." He broke off and looked up at last to see that Bertie was crying too. "But I love you. I love you more than I've loved anyone before. And I hope that's enough."

"Oh, petal," Bertie whispered. He slipped his hands out from under Pip's and guided Pip to sit on the sofa beside him. "It is more than enough," he said before he pulled Pip in for a kiss. It was tender and gentle and sweet, and more than a little teary.

Finally, when they pulled apart, Pip said, "Will you marry me? I don't think I actually said that part."

Bertie laughed and kissed him again. "There is nothing I'd like more."

Pip let Bertie wipe his face with a handkerchief before he buried his face in the crook of Bertie's neck and held him, knowing he finally had forever.

They sat in silence for a long while and Pip gradually came to realize that they'd have to talk about something, not the least of which was his proposal. He grudgingly sat up.

"You know," he said, "in my head, I never imagined that moment to be quite so soppy on my part."

Bertie chuckled. "Oh, I don't know. I thought it was most romantic, personally."

Pip situated himself on the sofa so he could lean against Bertie's shoulder. Then he pulled Bertie's hands to his lap and clasped them. "I'll leave the date up to you. I'm sure you have more knowledge of such things."

"I will gladly take care of the details."

Pip sighed, relieved. "I should tell you, I know nothing whatsoever about running a household."

Bertie kissed the top of his head. "I know you don't. I'll teach you everything you need to know. And I imagine Gavin will tell you a great deal as well. As soon as we tell Julian, they will be here in a trice, ready to teach you everything. And then, of course, my mother will want to visit for the wedding. And she will most certainly have advice, whether you want it or not."

"I'm very nervous about meeting her."

"Oh, darling, she will absolutely adore you. Trust me. I can predict exactly how she will react to meeting you. She will pronounce you adorable and beautiful. She will kiss you on both cheeks. She will tell you it's about time I settled down with a nice young man. And then she'll insist you call her Mother."

"She will? That's rather nice. I've never had a mother."

"And when you say *that*, dearest, she will proclaim you to be the most darling creature. And then she'll probably ask when we're having children and where we're going on our honeymoon. Cuts straight to the point, my mother."

Pip smiled even though Bertie couldn't see it.

"You know, I was thinking the trip we were discussing might make for a charming honeymoon. Don't you agree?"

Pip tilted his head up and kissed Bertie's cheek.

"Wonderful," Bertie said. "I'd hoped you might."

They went into lunch and chatted as they normally did. Only now, all their conversation was marked with little references of, "after we're married" and "oh, and for the wedding, I was thinking" and "when you move in." This was, of course, mostly from Bertie, but it pleased Pip to know that Bertie really had been looking forward to their marriage.

At one point, Pip reached forward to cover Bertie's hand and said, "I had thought your dinner party tomorrow might be a nice opportunity to announce our engagement. But I don't wish to overshadow the quizzing glass announcement."

Bertie blinked at him. "Good heavens, darling! What are you

talking about? Our engagement is of far more importance than the quizzing glass!"

Pip laughed and pulled Bertie's hand up to kiss the inside of his wrist.

After lunch, Bertie walked Pip to the stables to show him the horses.

"I'm not as great a rider as Charlie, of course. But I do like to ride. And I've made a few purchases of some nice mares on Charlie's recommendation. He told me what horses you've favored in his own stables and I bought some of similar temperament."

Pip gaped. "You bought horses for me?"

"Of course, my sweet. You can ride any of them here as often as you'd like. But the stablemaster can tell you which ones you're most likely to prefer."

Then they strolled through the garden and Bertie asked Pip if there was anything he wanted to change. There wasn't, but Pip enjoyed being asked. He began to see the house with new eyes, realizing that it would actually be his home soon and that he would know all of the servants by name and they would call him—

"My word," Pip said. "I won't be Mr. Standish anymore. What will I be?"

Bertie grinned at him. "Viscount Philip Finlington."

"A viscount?" Pip said. "Me? You cannot be serious, Bertie."

"Whyever not? I think Lord Pip Finlington has a very nice ring to it."

"Gerry's customers can't go around addressing me as 'my lord.' It wouldn't be fair."

"Oh, you'll just be known as the charmingly eccentric husband of the viscount who chooses to work in trade. Everyone loves you already anyway."

"Will Gerry be all right without me when we go on our honeymoon, do you think?"

"Of course she will," Bertie replied. "Actually, I confess I've been talking to her about it. The shop, I mean, not our honeymoon. I've been worried for quite some time that you two will run yourselves into the ground working nearly every day and for such long hours."

"Is that why you encouraged her to hire more help?"

"Well, that's one of the reasons, yes. But I also think it would do you both good to have at least two days off, perhaps three sometimes. She's already started training you and Seb to do the regular spell-building. There's no reason why the three of you can't divide the week up evenly so that you all have time to spend with your families." He glanced at Pip. "It wasn't entirely for selfish reasons. Gerry is married now and she will very likely want to have children of her own. I'm perfectly aware she can handle the shop and children, but it will be a good deal healthier for her to have the option to stay at home when she needs to without fretting about having to close the shop too."

Pip tilted his head in acknowledgement.

"And furthermore," Bertie went on. "Everyone knows that Laury intends to adopt as many children as he can fit into that little house. I think it will be good for Seb to keep busy with my work and the shop and the children, but it will be good if you two aren't depending entirely on him to be there every day."

"And me?" Pip said.

"Well, I should very much like to be able to take you away for a month or two on our honeymoon without feeling guilty," Bertie admitted. "And I do worry about you working too much. I always have, but it didn't make business sense to suggest anything. But the shop has been doing so well, Gerry was able to hire Seb, and could probably hire more help if she wanted.

Now she's gone off on her honeymoon and had to close the shop in her absence. I think it's high time we change the way we run it, that's all."

"And you told Gerry all this?"

"I told Gerry most of it," Bertie said. "I was not quite so eloquent on your part of it, but I suspect she understood."

"And she agreed?"

"She agreed to think about it. And she agreed that you and Seb ought to be fully trained up. I suspect that after some time of married life, she will be in agreement that a little additional time at home would be nice."

Pip chuckled.

After wandering amiably around the grounds for some time, they had tea and Pip poured out with Bertie giving tips and suggestions.

"Marvelously done, darling," he commended. Pip felt absurdly thrilled by the praise.

Bertie accepted his cup with a broad smile. "I was sure you'd pick it up quickly." He paused a moment. "Would you mind if I wrote to my mother and told her about our engagement? She'll be so pleased to know about it."

"Of course I don't mind," Pip said.

"I'm only worried because she'll want to come visit right away, you see."

"I am nervous about meeting her, but putting it off won't make it any less daunting. Please tell her as soon as you'd like."

Bertie kissed Pip's cheek. "Thank you, dearest. And Julian as well?"

Pip grinned. "I would be delighted to have them know."

"Good. They'll probably come down to visit too, you know."

"Excellent. They only just left and I miss them already. I fear that Charles and Gavin will likely know before dinner tomorrow. I'm sure I couldn't keep such a secret to myself when I go home tonight."

Bertie chuckled. "Charlie has always been the person who knew my secrets first. I don't mind it. He's good at keeping them." He sipped his tea. "Perhaps today and tomorrow we can look over the house together and see if everything is to your taste."

Pip blinked at him. "More than we've already done, you mean?"

Bertie inclined his head. "It is rather common for the one in charge of the household to do over the rooms according to their taste."

"That seems like a great deal of expense."

Bertie grinned and stroked Pip's cheek. "It is entirely up to you, of course. But if there is anything you'd like done over—a different paint color, a new piece of furniture, new paintings, anything at all—you've only to say the word."

Pip looked fondly at his friend—his fiancé. "You're going to spoil me dreadfully, aren't you?"

"Oh, darling, I cannot wait!"

Pip set his tea aside and leaned his head against Bertie's shoulder. "Have you already started thinking about when you'd like us to be married?"

"Well, I would like to wait long enough for Seb to be married, sweet thing. The dear boy will most certainly want to enjoy being the focus of everyone's attention for a little while. Laury has actually been working with Seb's parents to have everything ready when he returns from London. He wants to surprise him with a wedding date almost as soon as he gets home."

"Seb will love that," Pip said. "He's very impatient to be married."

"I can understand his excitement. I believe Laury intends to take him to London on their honeymoon for a fortnight—he and Charles and I have been discussing what they might enjoy doing there. All told, that will be about three or four months from now when they get back. I think that would be a fine time. Don't you?"

"That sounds perfect," Pip said. "Hopefully that's enough time for me to learn about household management."

"Oh, plenty of time to learn. And it does take a little while to get the paperwork and everything settled. I shall get started on that straight away so we have everything in order when we're ready. That will also give me time to prepare for our trip. I have a great many things I'd like to buy for us both in preparation, not to mention getting accommodations secured, and all of that nonsense."

"Do you think we could go on our honeymoon...well...Do you think we could stay here for a week or so after we're married?" Pip said tentatively. "I think I'd like to have this place as my home first before I leave it."

Bertie set his cup aside and then pulled Pip into a long kiss. "Whatever you want, darling."

After tea, Bertie led Pip around the first floor of the house, pointing out little things Pip might want to change or opportunities for adjustments. They ate dinner together, with Bertie explaining what each dish was. Then they retired to the sitting room for port and Pip made a more successful attempt at treating Bertie to a deep and passionate kiss. This time, Bertie obligingly cupped the back of Pip's head, exactly as Pip had wanted. By the end, they were both a little flushed and out of breath.

Bertie stroked through Pip's curly hair with gentle reverence. "I rather think it will be you who ends up spoiling me, dearest."

Pip smiled and leaned forward to whisper, "Oh, darling, I cannot wait!"

Then of course, Bertie had to pull Pip in for another long kiss. Afterwards, he said, "Are you going to start adopting terms of endearment? I must say I find the notion perfectly thrilling."

Pip laughed and curled up next to Bertie, leaning his head on the other man's shoulder. "I might. I do like to learn by example, you know. Practically everything I've done with you so far has been from observing how my friends treat their loved ones. Well," he added, glancing up at Bertie. "Not everything, of course."

"Yes," Bertie said with a chuckle. "I would be very much surprised if Gavin were *that* affectionate in front of others."

Pip paused. "I'm not sure when I'll be ready to be affectionate in front of others. Do you mind?"

"Of course not. Don't think I didn't notice the courage it took to take my hand the other day at lunch. I have no desire to see you uncomfortable. No one needs proof of our love, that's certain."

Pip smiled. "I think I'll get more accustomed to it eventually. I've never in my life felt so comfortable around others as I do with the people here. They make me feel so safe and so...I don't know...cared for."

"As ever, dearest, I will follow your lead on that front."

"I love you," Pip whispered up at Bertie.

Bertie looked down at him with a fond smile and stroked his cheek. "Your love is the greatest gift I could ever hope for, my darling," he said softly. He pulled Pip up for a light kiss. "I love you too."

Pip felt as though he could stay there forever, so he decided to take his leave before the desire got too great. Bertie walked Pip to the carriage door and Pip pulled him in for a final sweet goodnight kiss.

"Goodnight, my sweet," Pip whispered against Bertie's lips.

He felt Bertie smile against him. "Goodnight, petal."

Pip did not have to say a word when he walked into the house. Charles took one look at him and sprang up out of the sofa (amidst Gavin's irritable grumblings at the prompt removal of his bolster). "You did it?"

Pip nodded.

"Oh, my dear," Charles said, pulling Pip into a hug. "I knew you could do it."

Gavin came up to offer his own congratulations.

"We're going to announce it tomorrow night," Pip told them.

"Then I'll resist the temptation to insist you tell me everything," Charles said, beaming.

Pip laughed. "Don't worry, I'm sure everyone will be clamoring for information tomorrow." He ran a hand through his hair. "I was so terrified of it and now...I don't know that I've ever been so happy. It's exactly like you both said."

Charles wrapped an arm around both Gavin's and Pip's shoulders and led them all upstairs. "Love is like that."

"I suppose I can tell you that Bertie anticipates us being married in about three or four months—since it does impact both of you."

"Marvelous," Charles said. "Three more months of your splendid company."

"And that is certainly sufficient time to go over everything you might need to know," Gavin said.

"That's what Bertie said, too," Pip said.

Charles stopped at Pip's door. "Congratulations, my dear. I know you'll both be very happy. I couldn't be more pleased."

Pip wrapped them both in a hug—surprising himself and Gavin—and then wished them goodnight.

DAY SEVEN

The next morning, it took Pip a few moments to realize why he felt so full of bubbles and light. Then the previous day came rushing back to him. He grinned and threw his arms wide across the bed as if to welcome the day and all it might bring. He was going to marry Bertie. And while he still harbored some fears about the details of what that would entail, he found his joy and excitement far outweighed his concerns.

He went down to breakfast in high spirits. Charles grinned at him when he walked in but said nothing, proving Bertie correct in his ability to keep a secret. Gavin's mouth twitched, but he was inscrutable at the best of times. Seb greeted Pip as cheerfully as ever, completely unaware of the unspoken sentiments passing by in front of him.

"Laury and I received invitations to Bertie's for dinner tonight," he said as Pip helped himself to food. "Does that mean you two solved your puzzle?"

"We did. We'll tell you all about it tonight."

"Corking!" Seb said. He gulped down his tea.

"Oh, Seb, really!" Gavin said.

"I have to hurry," Seb said. "I overslept today. Why else would I have breakfast here?"

"Thank you very much for that," Gavin remarked drily.

Seb huffed and gave his brother a quick peck on the cheek. "Don't be like that, you goose. See you at dinner!" He left without waiting for a reply.

Gavin looked like he was trying very hard not to be pleased.

"And you thought he didn't care," Charles said, smiling at him.

Gavin rolled his eyes but didn't argue. He poured out for Pip. "How did the tea lessons go?"

"Very well," Pip said. "Bertie says I have a knack for learning."

"He's right," Charles said. "You picked up riding astonishingly fast."

"But he said he wants to teach me more. I suppose there's an order in who gets served first or something?"

Gavin nodded. "It is a little tedious, I'm afraid. But thankfully the rules apply to a great many situations. So knowing the order of precedence will be useful to know with seating arrangements at dinner parties and that sort of thing."

"Oh," said Pip. "I hadn't thought of that."

"Not your fault, my dear," Charles said. "Gavin and I are highly informal people. Even when we have company, we tend to disregard the rules as much as possible. As such, you've had little experience with those formalities."

"I'll teach you everything I know," Gavin assured him. "If *I* can manage, I haven't the least doubt that you will do just fine."

"Is that what you two will be doing today?" Charles said. "Order of precedence?"

"Maybe," Pip said. "He took me through the whole of the first floor yesterday to see if I might like to change anything. He mentioned wanting to do the same with the upper levels today."

Charles grinned. "He's very eager to have your stamp on the place, I think."

"But I don't have any preferences. I feel as though I'm letting him down when I don't really care what furniture we put in the green salon."

Charles laughed. "You'll come up with opinions eventually. Particularly when his mother arrives. She loves redecorating and will most certainly have all sorts of suggestions."

Pip ate and considered this. "The more I hear about her, the more I'm both nervous and intrigued."

"In-laws are like that," Charles said.

Gavin nodded. "I was as nervous as anything to meet Charles's aunt in Bath."

"What was she like?"

"Very formidable," Gavin said. "And very proper. But she did seem to approve of me."

"She adored you. She keeps asking when we're coming to visit. If you ask me, she's hoping I'll invite her to stay here for a little while."

Gavin tilted his head. "I think that would be nice. I quite liked her."

Charles gave his husband a wide smile. "How wonderful, my dear. I will write to her and tell her so."

A footman came in and delivered a note to each of them on a silver tray.

"Ah," Gavin said as he looked at his. "Gerry must have arrived home. Good."

Pip was surprised she had written to him as well.

Dear Pip,

I've missed you terribly and I cannot wait to see you. I saw that Bertie is having a dinner party tonight. If it were anyone else, I would probably complain of fatigue and not go. But considering Bertie is the host and everyone will be there, I will most certainly be there as well. And I shall be filled to the brim with stories of our trip so please prepare yourself accordingly.

I thought we might work a half day in the shop tomorrow. We won't open to customers unless someone comes to the door with an urgent need. I would like to check the inventory and make sure every-thing is ready for us to open the day after, so you needn't come in until after lunch. I'm sure I could do with the extra rest. It will be good to have a day in the shop with just us—partly because I enjoy your company, and partly because Bertie has been suggesting I adapt the store schedule. After spending a week alone with Basil, I confess I'm inclined to take his suggestions. But I don't wish to make any changes without your input. So we shall have much to discuss.

I hope you had a nice week away from the shop and I hope you were able to spend the time doing something pleasant.

I am looking forward to seeing you at dinner.

Affectionately,

Gerry

Pip smiled at the missive. He was amused that Bertie's predictions about Gerry's attitude toward the shop schedule turned out to be correct.

"Well," he said as he folded his note, "it would appear I'm due back in the shop tomorrow. So as much as I hate to sound like Seb, I'd better be off. This will be my last full day with Bertie before Sunday."

Charles grinned at him. "We'll see you tonight. And I'll have one of your suits sent over so you can change before dinner."

"Oh," Pip said. "Thank you. I suppose I ought to dress nicely, considering the occasion. That didn't occur to me."

"Well, we recently acquired that lovely embroidered waistcoat for you and there has been precious little opportunity for you to wear it. I fancy Bertie will quite like the way it looks on you."

Pip chuckled. "In that case, I will most certainly take your advice. Thank you, Charles."

He walked to Bertie's house with a deep sense of contentment. Gerry was back and he'd be returning to the shop. He was a little saddened to lose his full days in Bertie's company, but he also knew he would soon be able to spend every Sunday at home with him. If he understood Gerry's letter correctly, he would likely have more than Sundays at home in the near future.

Pip had never been one to look ahead to the future with anticipation. When he was younger, the need for survival was too important to waste time imagining possibilities. When he took up with Jack, he was too miserable to contemplate the future with anything but apprehension. When he moved to Tutting-on-Cress, he looked to the future with a sort of calm disinterest as he was perfectly satisfied to allow things to stay their normal course. But life, as it turned out, was not the sort of thing to stay a normal course. People changed, circumstances altered. Pip had seen such things happen for the better and the worse.

And now, for the first time, he was full of plans and dreams. The prospect of change excited him rather than alarmed him.

When he reached Bertie's house, he found Bertie was writing at his desk. Pip walked behind him, leaned over, and wrapped his arms around his neck and kissed his cheek. "Good morning, love."

Bertie stroked Pip's forearm. "Good morning, darling. How are you doing today?"

"I'm happier than I've ever been in my whole life. How are you?"

"I'm so glad to hear it. I am quite the same, actually." Bertie turned his head to plant a kiss on Pip's cheek.

"What are you doing?"

"Writing letters to Mother and to Julian," he replied. "I completely forgot to do it yesterday. I thought if I did it first thing, I wouldn't have to worry about remembering when I got carried away with the pleasure of your company."

"Perhaps I'd better take a walk around the garden while you finish?"

"I'm nearly done. No need to leave." So saying, Bertie patted Pip's arm and finished the letter he was writing.

As soon as he finished the letters and had properly sealed and addressed them, Bertie placed them on the end of his desk and leaned back into Pip's embrace. "You know," he said. "You keep surprising me with new ways with which you choose to show affection. I adore it."

Pip smiled. "I'm enjoying this exploration."

Bertie chuckled. "I know you learn by example. Who are we learning from today?"

Pip considered. "No one, actually. I just love seeing you sit at your desk, looking focused. You're adorable when you're intent, do you know?"

"Am I?" Bertie said softly.

"And every day that I've come in and found you thus, I've had a mad desire to greet you with a kiss. This seemed like an enjoyable way to do it."

"I quite agree with that assessment. Do I have your permission to return the favor when you have your own study set up?"

"Oh, most assuredly. I would be pleased as anything by it." He paused. "And perhaps when we're married, I might be able to distract you from your work, when I think you need it, of course."

"You think this isn't pleasantly distracting already?"

By way of response, Pip tilted his head and began pressing soft kisses to Bertie's jaw and then down his neck. He felt Bertie gasp and tighten his hold on Pip's arm. He stopped when he reached Bertie's crisp cravat. "I was thinking more along those lines, to be honest. What do you think?"

Bertie swallowed. "Oh, I think I should find that most enjoyable."

Pip didn't like the idea of teasing the man, so he straightened and slid his arms out from under Bertie's hands. Then he cleared away a spot on the desk and perched on the edge.

Bertie looked up at him, flushed and smiling.

Pip cupped Bertie's cheek with one hand. "Someday, I'd very much like to be able to sit in your lap. Either at your desk or on the sofa...or anywhere really. That one will take working up to, I'm afraid. Jack very much favored me on his lap."

Bertie's expression turned serious and he reached up to cover Pip's hand with his own. "I understand, darling."

"But I want you to know that it's something I intend to do eventually. I meant what I said yesterday. I want you to help me rewrite everything. He stole a great deal from me in his way. I don't like the idea of him stealing the joy I might get from sitting on your lap or your hands in my hair or you taking off my gloves after an evening out." He gave a small smile. "I was so very sad when he took my gloves off in that tavern. I had had so many stupid dreams of you doing it first."

Bertie nodded his understanding. "I would hardly be one to call those dreams stupid, Pip. And I will gladly help you rewrite everything. What's more, I will help you find new things to write, as it were. I'm confident we can find joy in a great many things together, as yet undiscovered."

Pip pushed himself off the desk and leaned over Bertie, kissing him tenderly. Afterward, he rested his forehead on Bertie's. "So, we need to see that your letters get sent off. And then what do you have planned for today?"

Bertie smiled. "As I said yesterday, I'd like to show you the rooms upstairs. There are a great many bedrooms and sitting rooms and nurseries and that sort of thing. I think it would be good for you to have an idea of the place."

"Very good," Pip said softly. "You know I'm going back to the shop tomorrow?"

"I do."

Pip grinned. "Gerry is already coming around to your way of thinking."

Bertie chuckled. "I thought she might."

With that, Pip straightened and let Bertie lead him out of the room. Bertie had not been wrong when he had described the upstairs section of the house as "a great many" rooms. For the most part, Pip couldn't really tell any of the rooms apart, with a few notable exceptions: Bertie's bedroom, the upper library, and the nursery. Pip was charmed by this last room. He wandered the bright space, trailing his fingers over a crib and a rocking chair. He picked up dolls and rattles. He held a carved wooden horse in his hand for a long moment, running his hands over the smooth wood.

Bertie came up behind him and wrapped his arms gently around Pip's waist. "All right there, darling?"

"Yes," Pip said slowly. "I never saw much of the Hartfords' baby when they came to stay. So this is the first time I've been in a nursery like this."

"Is it making you uncomfortable?"

Pip shook his head. "It's making me...I don't know how to put it...wistful, I suppose. So many lovely things. It feels odd to be surrounded by it when I..." He leaned against Bertie's chest. "I remember very little of my childhood, except that I was often lonely, often afraid, often hungry, often cold, and often running."

"Would you like to have children?" Bertie said softly.

"I don't know. I've never considered myself equal to the task, really."

"Well, as a couple in our position, it would not be particularly difficult. One hires nannies and governesses to help, you know. We wouldn't have to muddle through the experience on our own."

Pip nodded and put the horse down on a little table. "I don't wish to suggest we have children if you're opposed to having them."

"I'm not opposed to it," Bertie said. "We can consider the matter and decide after we've returned from our honeymoon, as it is a rather big commitment. We can wait years if you like. But I love children. And if you wished to adopt some, then I would gladly do so. Your happiness is my biggest priority, my sweet. You do know that?"

Pip turned back to smile at him. "I do. I shall think about it."

"As it happens," Bertie said. "There is an orphanage that I've heard about...I did some looking into it at one point. They take in children they find in the streets of London and try to get them settled in homes. Very progressive little establishment, from what I've seen. I quite liked it. Donated a good amount of money to it. So if you would like to take in some little ones, we can always—"

Pip cut him off with a kiss.

"You like the idea?" Bertie said with a smile after they broke off the kiss.

"I love it. Oh, Bertie, it would be quite perfect."

Bertie cupped Pip's face and stroked his cheek with his thumb. "We can save other little Pips from the same fate?"

Pip nodded, earnest. "There are so many of us."

"I know," Bertie said gently. "Perhaps two to start? They can keep each other company?"

Pip kissed Bertie again. "You really have been thinking about it, haven't you?"

"I wasn't at all sure of your preferences on the matter. But I wanted to have sufficient information for you, in any case. I learned of that place shortly after Nell moved in with me."

"You've been giving them money?" Pip said, smiling.

"For years now."

"Have I told you that I love you?"

Bertie grinned. "I never tire of hearing it."

Pip pulled Bertie in for another long kiss.

They spent the rest of the day in a leisurely fashion. They took a long, meandering walk around the garden and the conservatory. They had tea in the sitting room. An hour before the guests were expected to arrive, Bertie set up a spell in the larger drawing room, but didn't activate it.

Shortly after that, Pip's valet appeared with his suit, as Charles had promised. Bertie was surprised by it, but showed Pip to a large guest room, where he was able to freshen up and be dressed by his valet.

Charles turned out to be correct; Bertie was delighted by the sight of Pip in a nice suit and waistcoat. He stroked the embroidery. "Very fine work," he said. "We shall have to get you more of them."

Pip laughed. "I barely have occasion to wear this one."

"Well, as I've mentioned before, I anticipate a great deal of formal events in our future. Most of them will be after the honeymoon, of course, so there's plenty of time. But even before our marriage, and on our trip—well, it's good to be prepared, my sweet."

Charles and Gavin arrived first, bringing Seb and Laurence with them in their carriage. Charles could not stop smiling at Pip and Bertie, and Pip was very worried the man would burst with the knowledge before they'd made their announcement. Fortunately he didn't, and Seb was too distracted with talk of the garden expansion and wondering aloud what Bertie would explain the quizzing glass did. Pip was fairly sure Laurence had worked out the secret, if the young man's knowing smile was anything to go by. But Laurence was, it turned out, not nosy by nature, so he asked no prodding questions.

Gerry and Basil arrived some time later and for a while the talk was all about them and how well they looked and how their trip was and how good it was to see them. Gerry was keen to tell them everything.

Finally, Bertie brought everyone back to the drawing room. He fetched the quizzing glass, cast the spell, and then explained what he and Pip had discovered. He passed the quizzing glass around the room and everyone marveled at the novelty. Pip noticed that Bertie paid particular attention to how each person described the sight of magic and he suspected Bertie was already taking mental notes.

Dinner was called and they all adjourned to the dining room. The conversation ebbed and flowed and overlapped in the pleasant way it does when a group of people who like each other get together. They talked about Seb and Laurence's garden, about Pip and Bertie's quizzing glass project, and about Gerry and Basil's trip.

When everyone had eaten, Bertie leaned over to Pip and said in a low voice, "Would you like to do the honors, or shall I, dearest?"

"You do it, by all means," Pip said.

Bertie smiled and stood. "I had another reason for calling you all here today. Although I confess I did not know the reason when I sent out the invitations. I am pleased to let you all be the first to know that Pip and I are engaged to be married."

Everyone was very excited and offered their congratulations and asked when they were to be married. Bertie evaded answering with the exact date, saying only that he would be sure to keep everyone abreast of their plans.

At the end of the night, Pip left in the carriage with Charles, Gavin, and Seb. Gerry and Basil took Laurence in their carriage as he lived an easy distance from their house. Pip shared one brief, quiet moment with Bertie before climbing into the carriage. He was grateful that Charles and Gavin had ushered everyone out the door accordingly. Bertie took Pip into his arms and gave him a sweet and tender kiss goodnight.

Pip climbed into the carriage to see all three men grinning at him expectantly.

"You were right," he said to Gavin. "It was decidedly worth it."

As the carriage made its way down the road, Pip looked out the window at the grand house, realizing that he already considered it home. He had, in fact, long considered it home, at least to some extent, for it was home to the man who held his heart.

Pip sat back in his seat, feeling satisfied with life, feeling surrounded by love, and feeling hopeful for the future in all its many possibilities.

The End

CAN'T GET ENOUGH cozy Regency fantasy? Check out the first book in my next series, co-authored with S.O. Callahan: *Breeze Spells and Bridegrooms*!

NOTE FROM THE AUTHOR

Dear Reader,

I drafted this story years ago, before *The Education of Pip* had been released. I wrote it before I'd even written Gerry's book. I've known for a long time that Pip and Bertie deserved a satisfying conclusion to their love story. I hope I've provided you with one.

I have two more stories partially drafted for this series. However, in my tendency to rush from one project to the next, I pushed myself into burnout. This series started to become a chore rather than a joy. So as much as I hate to do it, this story will serve as a temporary ending to *Meddle & Mend*. I hope to return to it someday soon.

In the meantime, I hope you will take a chance on some of the stories I've written with S.O. Callahan. In them you will find similar tales of love, found family, and self-acceptance.

This series has meant so much to me. These books pushed me as a writer, helped me find some wonderful friends, and acted as a crash course on indie publishing. I've learned so much and I'm so grateful to everyone who found these stories.

Thank you for following along on this journey. I hope to take us all back to Tutting-on-Cress again before too long. In the meantime, I remain

Affectionately yours,
Sarah Wallace

Acknowledgments

As ever, this book came to life thanks to my own found family. To Ashley, thank you for being one of the first and last people to read my stories. To my alpha and beta readers, Alexis, Katie, Shannon, Meg, Sebastian, and Tessa, thank you for all of your valuable feedback! To my editor, thank you for all of your valuable feedback and for sticking with me throughout this series!

And to my incredible readers, thank you for continuing to read my stories! I couldn't do this without any of you!

Editor: Mackenzie Walton
Proofreader: Ashley Scout
Front cover photo by Annie Spratt via Unsplash
Back cover photo by Katherine Hanlon via Unsplash
Author photos by Toni Tillman

ABOUT THE AUTHOR

Sarah Wallace lives in Florida with their cat, more books than she has time to read, a large collection of classic movies, and an apartment full of plants that are surviving against all odds. They only read books that end happily.

ALSO BY SARAH WALLACE

MEDDLE & MEND: A REGENCY FANTASY SERIES

Letters to Half Moon Street - Read Gavin's story

One Good Turn - Read Nell's story

The Education of Pip - Read Pip's story

Dear Bartleby - Read Seb's story

The Spellmaster of Tutting-on-Cress - Read Gerry's story

The Glamour Spell of Rose Talbot - *Meddle & Mend* Prequel - Free to all newsletter subscribers!

FAE & HUMAN RELATIONS: A REGENCY FANTASY SERIES BY SARAH WALLACE & S.O. CALLAHAN

Breeze Spells and Bridegrooms - Book 1 in *Fae & Human Relations* - Read a sneak peek now!

Fire Spells Between Friends - Book 2 in *Fae & Human Relations*

Shade Spells with Strangers - Book 3 in *Fae & Human Relations*

Cleaning Spells Before Courtship - Book 4 in *Fae & Human Relations*

Protections Spells for Press Buildings - Free to all newsletter subscribers!

POWELL PRODUCTIONS: A GOLDEN AGE OF HOLLYWOOD FANTASY SERIES BY SARAH WALLACE & S.O. CALLAHAN

When I'm in Your Arms

Together on Parade

SIGN UP FOR MY NEWSLETTER!

Are you signed up for my newsletter? Join now at sarahwallacewriter.com to be in the know!

Newsletter subscribers are the first to see book covers, receive the first chapter of new releases a month before release date, get sneak peeks at preorder campaign art, and a free novelette! I've also been known to send deleted scenes or scenes in alternate POV and I plan to do more of that!

PREVIEW FOR BREEZE SPELLS AND BRIDEGROOMS

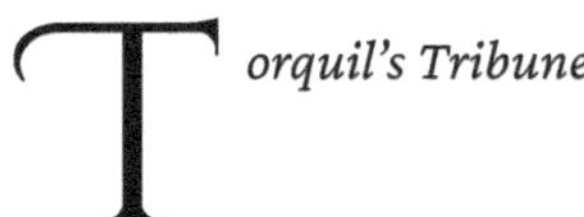

orquil's Tribune

Greetings fair folk and haphazard humans,

For those just now returning to London, welcome back.

Did you miss me?

The summer months are always horrifically dull for this humble writer. So little gossip to share. So little havoc to wreak. We are excessively relieved to see people return to the city. Whose lives shall be changed this Season? Who will fall in love? Who will flirt with scandal? We are, as ever, eager to find out.

It would appear that the Council for Fae & Human Magical Relations is preparing to convene soon, a whole month before the Season begins. To what do we owe the pleasure of a group of blustery and generally useless politicians to our fair city?

Well, the trend of human children receiving low scores on their Hastings Exam has started to reach a crisis point. Low scores have always been a potential result of the magical testing process, but high scores are becoming increasingly rare. As more and more humans with low Hastings scores reach adulthood, we are seeing the strain on society.

This strain is not caused by those with low scores but rather the way the world treats them. We are seeing more humans rejected for employment opportunities, or reaching the age of majority without a single marriage proposal. As human children are increasingly less likely to receive the desired score, this presents a troublesome insight into our future.

Will the Council find a solution? This writer considers it unlikely. But who knows? Perhaps a hero will emerge from the midst. It hasn't happened since King Arthur's reign but, as they say, nothing is impossible where magic is concerned.

Your esteemed editor,

Torquil Pimpernel-Smith

Roger

ROGER BARNES ATTEMPTED to surreptitiously dab at the beads of sweat gathering on his forehead. The Council's chambers were notoriously hot, even in the waiting area. Some blamed it on the heated debates between councilmembers, but Roger privately believed it had more to do with the placement of the wing. It really did get the most atrocious amount of sunlight. Convening in late summer did not help. Roger had a brief wistfulness for his family's country estate, wind gliding over the pond as he read by a tree. He shook his head and reined in his thoughts. Now was not the time for wistfulness.

He took his notes out of his pocket, reading them for what felt like the hundredth time. The paper was crumpled from so much handling. He didn't need to read the notes; they were memorized already. But he tended to get flustered when he was nervous, agitated, or generally upset. Quite frankly, flustered was practically Roger's natural state. He folded the paper, his hands shaking. He put it back in his pocket, decided he ought to have it handy just in case, and pulled it out again. He tapped the paper against his thigh, decided that wasn't doing the crumpled state any favors, put it back in his pocket, and clenched his hands together.

He could hardly believe he was doing this *again*. Was he really foolish enough to approach the Council for a third time? When an aide appeared at the door and beckoned him in, he concluded that, apparently, he was foolish enough to do just that.

He felt six pairs of eyes follow his progress into the room. He had always believed that an even number of members was an absurd way to assemble a council responsible for big decisions, but no one cared much about his opinions on the subject. In this case, his reasons for approaching were so important that

Roger felt overwhelmed by it all. He walked up to the little stand and placed his wrinkled notes down, smoothing out the edges. He looked up and found his father sitting at the end of the table, the lowest-ranking human councilmember, and the only person in the group that did not thoroughly intimidate Roger.

"Well, Mr. Barnes," Councilmember Williams said, his gruff voice making Roger feel even smaller, "to what do we owe the pleasure this time?"

He tried to hide his wince. He glanced at his father, who gave him an encouraging smile. He cleared his throat, "Thank you, sir. I am grateful for the opportunity to approach this august company again." He could tell his voice sounded monotone as he read out the words, but monotone was preferable to stuttering, so he kept going. "I understand that the Council is working to find a solution to the...Hastings score... situation and I-I would like to offer a suggestion."

Councilmember Cricket glanced at Roger's father. "Yes," she mused. "I suppose you would have opinions about that."

"I hope it is different from your last suggestion," Councilmember Gibbs sniffed. "Your last one left much to be desired."

His last suggestion—to raise the testing age to eighteen— had been squashed in record time. It was a pity. He'd really believed in that one. However, he had been significantly less prepared when he'd approached the Council before. His reasoning behind changing the testing age had not been well argued. Perhaps now that the situation was more dire, the Council would be more willing to hear his solution—particularly when his notes were better organized.

"To be fair," Councilmember Applewood put in, "the previous suggestion was not a bad one. But I'm still concerned about keeping families in suspense about inheritance for so long. It would be very taxing, particularly for the children involved."

"Not to mention, valuable time would be wasted that could be spent training heirs in what they need to know," Councilmember Williams added.

"There is little need to go over the subject again," Councilmember Wrenwhistle said coolly. "I take it Mr. Barnes has a different solution in mind this time."

"Y-yes," he stammered. "My proposal is to move away from the Hastings Examination rubric altogether."

There was, predictably, a small clamor at that, mostly from the human side, although there were a couple of fae members who were chattering too. He thought they seemed approving. Councilmember Applewood was looking at him pensively, a smile playing upon her lips. Roger felt a small bit of hope at that expression.

Councilmember Wrenwhistle raised her hand to silence the rest. "That is certainly a bold suggestion. I am curious to hear your reasons and what you suggest as an alternative."

"Well," he said. "My reasons are fairly simple, I think. As you know, the success rate for the Hastings Exams are extremely low. Some families see children with no passing rates at all, even from powerful bloodlines. My belief is that the exam is too narrow in its observations to be properly conclusive. My proposal..." he shifted his notes so the second page was on top, "is to have a more nuanced approach to testing. We only test human children on one spell. If we were to broaden the scope of the examination, we could test multiple strengths at once. I do not have a new model fully drafted yet, but I believe testing for...er...spell force, as we currently do, but also control, attention to detail, and...creativity, would be beneficial."

Councilmember Williams scoffed. "Creativity? What, are we going to have students offer up poems to their examiners?"

"N-no, sir. But it would be good to see students apply principles of basic theory to multiple spells. Sort of a theoretical examination on top of a practical one."

"Roger," his father said, his tone mild, "what do you propose for the fae examinations? I agree that the Hastings Exam may be out of date, but it is the most standard form of testing we have and has the benefit of being the most closely aligned to the fae test, the Sciurus Exam. Both rubrics must be comparable."

"I admit, sir, that I do not have sufficient expertise on fae magic," Roger said. "I would cede to the Council on that part, although I do agree that it is an important part of the issue."

"It hardly matters what the testing rubrics are," Councilmember Cricket sneered. "*We* do not treat our children like outcasts when they don't do well. I think that is the most critical issue at hand."

His father looked like he wanted to agree but Gibbs was quick to say that the fae had issues of their own, thank you very much. Then Cricket argued that whatever issues the fae had, they at least protected their own, which could not be said for humankind.

Roger felt himself wilt a little. This was more or less what happened the first time. He had made a proposal that started a debate, then he had been unceremoniously sent out. It wasn't quite as bad as the second time, when he suggested the testing age be altered. That time he had practically been laughed out of the room. He supposed if he had to choose, watching the Council descend into its usual chaos was somewhat preferable.

Wrenwhistle raised her hand again. The arguing died down, primarily because the fae were pointedly respectful to their Head of Council and the humans couldn't very well argue against silence. When the bickering stopped, she was silent for a long moment before saying, "Your proposal has merit, Mr.

Barnes." Roger felt hope kindle in his chest. "But," she went on, quickly extinguishing that brief feeling, "a vague idea is not sufficient. We will give you a fortnight to come up with a detailed proposal, a workable testing rubric. I agree that a comparable model for testing fae magic is necessary, although I appreciate your restraint in overstepping beyond your expertise." Roger thought this was said with some sarcasm but he tried to pretend it wasn't. "So for now we will give you an opportunity to present to us a real solution. Something we can act upon. If your rubric is accepted, we will assign a fae to work with you on a comparable rubric for fae magic. Are we in agreement, Councilmember Williams?"

Williams gave Roger a long look. Finally, he nodded. "I believe that will suffice."

"Thank you, Mr. Barnes."

Roger knew a dismissal when he heard one and wasted no time in leaving. Once outside the room, he allowed himself to process his warring emotions. On one hand, they actually listened to him and hadn't laughed at him outright! That was certainly progress. On the other hand...he had not figured on developing the testing rubric himself. He had ideas, but with his Hastings score, he didn't have much hope that those ideas would be taken seriously. However, his mind was already starting to churn. He strode down the hall, lost in thought.

Wyn

AT ONE POINT IN TIME, Wyn supposed, the grandeur of the Parliament buildings along the Thames had been quite impressive. Countless spires stretched from the rooftops, tall enough to pierce the dreary, unwelcoming clouds that often collected overhead. Inside, the ogive arches helped draw attention to the stained-glass windows and intricate stonework on the walls and high ceilings. It was easy to let your jaw go slack at such a spectacle if you were not accustomed to it.

Wyn had been visiting his grandmother in the Council's chambers his entire life, effectively numbing him to the beauty of the architecture. Even the meticulously manicured grounds that surrounded him on his brisk walk along the cobbled path had long since faded into familiarity.

He followed his older brother Emrys up the steps, who touched his fingers to the brim of his hat as he greeted the door-keepers by name.

"*Ugh*," Emrys moaned as they passed through the vestibule, quick to voice what both men were thinking. "Could it possibly be any hotter?" Even the echoing of their footsteps in the long hallway seemed muffled by the stifling air inside the building.

Wyn struggled to ignore the way the damp fabric of his cravat was sticking to his neck. His discomfort wasn't enough to make him regret wearing his thick, wavy hair long enough to reach his shoulders, though. It was a decision he'd made just recently, opting to let it grow out of the more fashionable cut that most men were wearing. His mother could protest many of his decisions, but this would not be one of them.

He took a deep breath and let it out in an impatient sigh.

"I just hope Grandmother makes this quick," he muttered, still trailing behind Emrys toward the chambers. There was an invitation to the first event of the Season with his name on it sitting atop his dressing table. He would wear something far less stuffy than his high boots and heavy coat. With any luck, the evening would dissolve into a more private situation that required no clothing at all.

"When has she ever been known to do that?" Emrys asked with a faint chuckle. "Although, maybe if I show her the way my new clothes are being ruined with sweat stains, she'll take pity and grant us leave."

As they approached the final corner in the maze of window-lit hallways, someone called Emrys' name. Both men turned to look over their shoulders and discovered the familiar smile of Keelan Cricket, one of Emrys' closest friends and the son of another councilmember.

"Go ahead, I'll catch up with you in a moment." Emrys left no room for argument as he pivoted and took off in the direction they'd just come. Wyn rolled his eyes, knowing that was the exact opposite of the truth, and turned the corner—directly into someone else.

"Watch it," Wyn hissed, taking a steadying step backward, trying his best to maintain appearances in case his brother or anyone else had seen. Upon realizing who had run into him, his annoyance flared. Of *course* it would be Barnes getting in his way.

"Apologies," the shorter man mumbled, his hands doing a ridiculous little dance, as though he couldn't decide between reaching for the scraps of paper he'd dropped on the floor or fixing his spectacles that had fallen askew after crashing into Wyn's chest.

Wyn crossed his arms and watched as Roger bent to pick up

the papers from where they had fluttered to their feet. His mouth curled into a faint smirk.

"Had to draw yourself a map to find the exit, did you?"

Roger righted himself with a puff of an exhale and quickly folded his papers away into a pocket, fixing his spectacles with an indignant glare. Wyn's gaze slid down to the man's shoes and back up again. Barnes had never known how to dress for his plump figure, nor find a suitable color palette to match the light brown of his skin. Such a pity.

"I've been here just as many times as you, Wyndham," Roger said. Wyn bristled instantly at the casual use of his name. "I know my way around—"

"You will call me Mr. Wrenwhistle," Wyn ground out with a slow emphasis on each word, his jaw tight. The man was a year older than he was, but the fact remained that he wouldn't tolerate the disrespect of being addressed by his first name in public, especially by the likes of Roger Barnes. They might've known each other since they were children, but that did not make them friends.

He felt it then, the familiar tingling, and Wyn knew his magic was seconds away from begging to be set free. It was an issue he'd dealt with for as long as he could remember. Returning to London was most stressful for a fae who struggled with being surrounded by disorder. For Wyn, his melancholy was exacerbated by the stress, resulting in his magic demanding to be felt as his emotions flared.

Wyn drew in a deep, silent breath and held it, eyes sliding shut. He focused on what he could feel. The growing ache in his chest from holding the sweltering air in his lungs. The perspiration clinging in some unmentionable places. The cool, smooth metal of the rings on his fingers. He exhaled as these thoughts filtered through his mind, quelling the surge of emotion that had dared to unwind him right there in the hall.

"Are you...feeling quite the thing?"

The sound of Roger's voice, laced with just enough concern to sound sarcastic, washed away every speck of control Wyn had just regained.

"Do get out of my way," he said brusquely, stepping around Roger and continuing down the corridor.

The heels of Wyn's boots clacked harder than necessary all the way to the final door that separated him from the Council's chambers. He slammed through it with a flourish, coat whipping about his hips as he went. Without needing to read the nameplates hanging outside the offices, Wyn approached his grandmother's and let himself in.

Iris Wrenwhistle lifted her gaze from the papers on her desk, a pleasant look of surprise on her face despite the fact that she'd been the one to request his presence. This was the way she always regarded her grandchildren. She treated every interaction with them like a small gift.

"There you are, darling," she said with a warmth that helped wash away the last of Wyn's twist of frustration. "Where is your brother?"

"Chatting up a friend," he replied. The chair by the window had always been his favorite. He plunked into it like a sullen teenager and crossed his arms over his chest, eyes cast to the floor.

"Ah, yes. It's good to be back in London with everyone, is it not? A little early, but we've got important work to do."

I hate it here, he wanted to tell her. *I hate it more than anything.*

Wyn wanted to be back in the country where he could enjoy the fresh air and sunshine and nights under the stars without the constant bustling and noise of high society. Somewhere he was not continually reminded that, despite his magical aptitude, he was inferior in the eyes of others thanks to the score he'd been given when he was just a child.

"It's good to be back," he agreed, though the lie burned hot on his tongue.

WANT to read more of Breeze Spells and Bridegrooms? Buy it now!

9 781737 432760